T0096149

On Cedar Hill

Emil Kresl

Amberjack Publishing
New York, New York

Amberjack Publishing
228 Park Avenue S #89611
New York, NY 10003-1502
http://amberjackpublishing.com

Publisher's Cataloging-in-Publication data

Kresl, Emil.
On Cedar Hill / Emil Kresl.
pages cm
ISBN 9780692487129 (pbk.)
ISBN 9780692501481 (ebook)

1. Families --Fiction. 2. Dysfunctional families --fiction. 3. Minnesota --Social Life and Customs --Fiction. 4. Domestic fiction. I. Title.

PS3611 .R468 O53 2015
813.6 --dc23   2015948084

Cover Design: Cold Milk Creative
Printed in the United States of America

For Mom

Contents

Part One: Cocktails

Repartee

That evening, for whatever reason, I was obsessed with Wexler's lawn. I tried obstinately to speak with him about it, its argyle cut and the density of the turf, but he was always somehow otherwise occupied. "Donovan," I said at one point as we crossed paths in the throng, "who does your lawn for god's sake, Burberry? No, it must be St. Francis himself!" Alas, he was intercepted by another guest eager for his ear. It was a blissfully typical gathering on Cedar Hill, happy neighbors standing shoulder-to-shoulder, plying pale-colored drinks to-and-fro. The lulls in laughter were filled with the rhythmic puhk-puhk of the tennis courts in the distance, likely the Jagger boys having it out again. Yet, I could not, regretfully, let go of that lawn, shouting after our host, "No, Donno! It could only have been a NASA engineer to calculate and realize the exactitude of those lines! It's a goddamn marvel." As Donovan made his retreat, he nearly flattened the little Larsen girl—christened Sissy, poor thing—who was wearing a navy blue one-piece with the stars and stripes stretched across her puerile belly. In her arms, clearly against its will, was the Peterburg's cat, Norma, "After Norma Desmond in *Sunset Boulevard*," Audrey Peterburg would be damned sure to have you know.

I was after old Donovan when Becks, my spit-fire

3

bride, set her pick out of nowhere. "Look, Johnny," says the wife, "why don't you take it easy for awhile? Switch to Coke for the next hour maybe?"

"What's the problem, Becks? Wexler and I are just talking yard. Must seem awfully silly, but not to worry, dear. Just boys being boys."

"All the same, Johnny, I think poor Donovan might not be in the mood to chat about his lawn this evening. Maybe it's just a sore spot at this particular—"

"Donovan!" I shouted across the party, turning a good number of heads. "Are you sensitive about your grass, old buddy? Becks here seems to think you might be put off about me being impressed with your goddamn lawn. Isn't that just a hoot? Women! Isn't that right, Donovan?"

What a painful thing, to look back on one's actions and be ashamed. I couldn't even see the man, for goodness sake. Instead, I saw only Sissy Larsen who, still with an armful of cat, had made her way up on the diving board, staring intently into the chlorinated water cluttered with toys. Norma was known to be an extraordinary animal as far as that sort of thing goes. As I recall, the Peterburgs bragged that it was something called a tortoiseshell Persian, with a luxurious coat running from sandy to chocolate brown and a flash of tangerine over yellow eyes. Apparently a real gem for those in the know.

Here, as I pondered just what little Sissy's intentions were with Norma, Donovan's woman Melissa came over to have a few choice words with me, her whiskey sour coming at me. "Listen, Johnny, Becks is just trying to keep you from making such a damned ass of yourself. You've been going on all night about the fucking lawn. Yes, we realize it's a nice lawn. But Jesus, Johnny, let it go already. I mean really."

"Well pardon me all to hell, Melissa." Yes, I'm mortified to even think of it, but this is the tone I used. "Just excuse me all to hell for paying you the compliment of appreciating the absolute remarkable beauty of your lawn. Has it come to that? Have we all reached the point in our community that to recognize the hard work and craftsmanship of one another's homes is forbidden? Are we all that jaded, Mel, that now we must pretend that such feats of horticultural magnificence are mundane? Well, I sincerely apologize, but I cannot—that's right, I am simply incapable of ignoring such pristine majesty." And here two things happened: one, Sissy with a dramatic gesture one might use to release a ceremonial dove, tossed Norma into the pool; and two, sweet, dear, cunning Becky spilled her drink on my crotch, feigning utter embarrassment and regret, but I know all too well it was intentional.

"God, what a fool," she said. "I'm so, so sorry, Johnny. God, I'm such a klutz."

"Sure, Becks, nothing but a little accident, I'm sure. How could I begrudge you that, right? But listen, the Larsen girl just tossed the Peterburg's cat into the drink." The poor thing had clearly never been involved with quite so much water and didn't know what to do with it all. With her gorgeous fur now sodden,

Norma seemed barely a cat at all. More of an unsettling sock-puppet of sorts. She struggled to save herself by sinking her claws into a kickboard, but every time Norma looked as if she might be able to hoist herself to safety, the board flipped and sent her back under.

"Thanks for understanding, Johnny. Now let's get you home and out of those trousers before people think you've wet yourself."

"Right, Becks. How very thoughtful of you to worry about what people think of me." Melissa had her hand to her mouth at this point, hiding not at all her devious smile. Undoubtedly, she and Becky would have a good laugh at my expense the next day. "But I'm perfectly fine standing out here with a pair of wet balls, dear. Not a disgrace to yours truly, for I don't mind what others might think of me. Especially when I know I'm amongst such true blue friends. Now, let's do something about that drowning cat."

"Oh, come on. Really, Johnny. I don't want you to be uncomfortable. We can come back over when you've changed."

"But I don't want to change. I'm just fine the way I am, don't you think?"

"No, Johnny. No, I don't think you're fine. You're soaking wet. It's indecent. Please, Johnny, just come home for god's sake."

"Take it easy, Becks. Tell you what, just let me take care of Norma and have a few words with Donovan, and we can head out in a matter of minutes. How's that sound?"

"Who's Norma and why do you need to talk to Donovan? What do you have to say to him that can't wait? I think he's tied up with the Van Pelts right now anyway. Let's just head out and then you can talk to him when we get back."

It was true enough. There he was, standing poolside, chatting away with Peg and Richard Van Pelt while Norma the sinking cat—not ten feet away—began giving up the fight. Sissy, from her exalted position, little fists to her hips, seemed the only person to take any notice of Norma's predicament.

"Tied up, Becky? Hah. Pals like old Donovan and myself are never tied up with other people." He cut a remarkable figure there, his Bulgari watch, Napa chardonnay, and glorious teeth shimmering in the light of a Tiki torch while the cat splashed in the background.

"Look, Johnny. What do I have to do?"

"What do you mean?"

"Would you like me to fix you something to eat at home? Do you want sex? How about a blowjob? How does that sound? We'll go home and when you get out of those wet pants I'll give you a nice blowjob."

"Good Lord, Becky, please. You're making a scene." And off I went toward the pool, the tribulations of Norma still ineffective in catching anyone else's attention. But on the way, who should I run into but the Peterburgs, an aged but regal couple of the hill. "Audrey! Tom! Thank God." They said nothing. In fact, their smiles dissolved as I spoke. "It's Norma! She's in the pool."

"Ridiculous," said Tom.

"Norma despises the water," said Audrey.

"Yes, but—"

"Please, Johnny, we're right in the middle of something here."

So off I went to rescue Norma myself and have a word with Donovan Wexler, but as I arrived I found that I was too late for the former. Norma lay buoyed but defeated amidst all the happy floaties. Sissy, now prostrate on the diving board, a vacant look on her face, studied the corpse.

Onward then: "Hey, there, kids! Monopolizing our generous host, are you?"

"Hello, Johnny," said Richard flatly. Peg took her drink in both hands and dropped her shoulders.

"Richard! Peg! Goddamn, it's good to see you two." I took them both into an embrace and whispered, "Do you know how much I love these evenings? The noodles in the swimming pool, the citronella in the air, the gin and tonic coursing through my veins."

"Yes, Johnny," said Richard, pulling himself away. "We love these evenings too."

"But do you really, Richard? Do you really appreciate how fucking lovely it is?"

"Would you mind watching the language, Johnny?" asked Peg. "The boys are running around. As are some other children."

"Ah, the boys! God, I love those kids. How are the twins doing these days?"

"They're fine, thank you."

"Johnny," said Donovan, "I think you've wet yourself."

"Are they, Peg? Because I ran into Dr. Moldenower at the hospital and he said their insides were in dire straits." Peg and Richard exchanged a look. "Not that that's not par for the course with Down syndrome, mind you."

"Johnny, why are you talking to Dr. Moldenower about our boys?"

"Well, I'm a doctor, Richard. That's what we do. At least good doctors do. We inquire after our patients. And as you two are my dear friends, I'm especially concerned."

"Yes, well—" began Richard, but was interrupted by a red-faced Peg.

"Their feet, Johnny! That's all you need be concerned about, thank you. When we've got an ingrown toenail, Johnny, you'll be the first fucking podiatrist we call!" Then she stormed off.

"Why don't you call it a night," said Richard, then followed after his wife.

"Mel!" shouted Donovan. "Could you get those pool fellows on the horn, dear?"

In our bedroom, as I struggled with my clammy trousers, I called to Becks for some assistance. "Might I get a hand here, Becks?"

"Don't be gross, Johnny." No matter though, for after falling to the floor, I was eventually able to manage myself.

"What did you say to the Van Pelts, Johnny?"

"We'll talk in the morning, Becks. I'm beat."

"Was it something about the twins? God, Johnny, please tell me it wasn't about the boys." Into the hamper the pants went—or at least in that general vicinity—and under the sheets I crawled while Becky stood before me with her hands to her hips, just like little Sissy observing her dying cat.

"Come on, Becks. You know how much I love those kids."

"I do. What did you say, Johnny?" And off the sheet went with a mighty snap from the wife.

"I told them I had heard from Moldenower about their intestinal problems."

"How's that?"

"They're going to need catheters."

"What the hell were you doing talking to Moldenower about the Van Pelts?"

"We ran into each other."

"And in passing you asked about the boys."

"It wasn't really in passing."

"Clear it up, Johnny."

"It was during some downtime. I was forced into conversation."

"Downtime. At the hospital."

"We were waiting for an MRI to run the course."

"Both of you? Why?"

I sat up here and patted the bed for Becky to have a seat. She obliged, as I knew she would. A wonderful wife, that Becky. "It was on me. The MRI I mean, Becks. As it turns out, I've had quite a few tests of late."

"What the hell are you talking about, Johnny?"

"Not much, sweetie. Hate to worry you, but it seems I may have caught the big C."

Speechless, as you might imagine. In hindsight, I suppose it wasn't the best way to spring it on poor Becky, but then, is there a good way?

"Sorry I didn't tell you sooner, Becks, it's just that I didn't want to send out a false alarm and have everyone—"

"No."

"Sorry?"

She shook her head with a troubled sort of smile at her lips. "You've had too much to drink," she said.

"Now look," I said, "sweetie. There's a bit in the kidney, and a bit in the bowel, but I believe—"

"You should get some sleep," said the wife, then got up from the bed and switched out the light at the wall.

"Becks," I called after her, but oddly enough the woman just walked right out of the room. Right out of the house, in fact, and kept on walking.

Holzkind

Our neighborhood, Cedar Hill, is not a suburb. We are an affluent, tasteful and revered community within Minneapolis. The people of Cedar Hill are singular in our good taste. We are not the type that spend money like they've just won a lifetime shopping spree at Walmart or the local boat emporium. We handle our wealth with a certain aplomb, and Cedar Hill as a whole reflects that sophistication. Even the things that some might see as imperfections, a crumbling stone wall, or a lightning struck elm, are looked upon not as defects, but rather a kind of character that we are able to not only embrace, but allow to shine as yet another enviable feature of our little community.

Holzkind is another example of our ability to extract the positive from what, to the less refined or receptive, might seem negative. Because Cedar Hill abuts the Great Northern Railroad, we are occasionally visited by transients. This is not a problem. These men (and, interestingly enough, sometimes women) can emigrate just as quickly as they immigrate. They find that handouts are not readily given here, and our law enforcement is eager to make it clear that they are not welcome on Cedar Hill. But a tramp we would come to know as Holzkind was not so easily discouraged. He instead took up residence on Cedar Hill in various undisclosed places, perhaps in the heavily wooded park that sits in the heart of the neighborhood, or certainly in the brush beside the railroad where he was often spotted rummaging about in the tall grass. What was he doing there, people wanted to know? What could he possibly be looking for in the reeds along the railroad? Yes, there were those on Cedar Hill who didn't like the idea of having this man around. They would manufacture scenarios of what he *might* do, or what he *could* be capable of. But I saw Holzkind for what he was: a self-sufficient and adventurous spirit; a man who was able to somehow sustain himself without succumbing to the boundaries and burdens of normal society.

Not three days following Donovan's soiree, with the wife still MIA, as I was driving home from the hospital (not from work but a treatment which Dr. Inertis merrily called a chemo cocktail), I saw Holzkind coming from our corner store. He was unwrapping a candy bar—a Charleston Chew I think—while trying to support a large paper sack under one arm. I parked my Tahoe in front of the Larsens' and joined Holzkind on foot.

"Hello there, friend," said I, but Holzkind was not immediately responsive to my overtures. "Hello there, hello there. May I have a brief word with you, sir?" Here, as I got within three feet of the man, he froze, staring at me from the corner of his eye like a nag too worn out to bolt.

"Sorry. So sorry to bother you. Won't take a minute. Just a quick question if you don't mind." Still no movement from Holzkind until I put out my hand which he eventually accepted.

"John Gingham. Sorry I haven't introduced myself earlier. Rude of me, I know. Holzkind, isn't it? Didn't catch your first name, though." He still didn't offer it.

"Right," I forged on, "doesn't matter anyway, does it? Just wanted to stop briefly to see if you might have an interest in helping me in the yard a bit. Nothing too strenuous. Just some clipping and digging here and there. Maybe the occasional stone to transport. I'll be more than fair on salary, perhaps with a bonus now and again, if it's warranted. What do you say?"

There was silence for a good while, but I could see that Holzkind was churning it out, so I let him be. I've dealt with the dull mind in my practice now and again. The aged or chemically abused. I know to give them their time to allow the information to settle into the appropriate pockets of the mind and it finally did happen with Holzkind of course. But his response was rather unexpected. In fact, I must say it was just slightly disturbing. This man who, before that day, seemed to live his life entirely within his own mind and, as far as I can remember, never once made eye contact with me, said to me, "The yellow split-level on Idyll Drive, right?"

And suddenly I was the one trying to get the information to settle into the proper pockets. My mouth was open, but for a few seconds I was unable to find the words.

"Why, yes, in fact that is the one," I finally said.

"But it's really a Cotswold Cottage and more of a maize color—"

"You need me now?" he asked.

"Oh, no. I was thinking perhaps tomorrow morning if that might suit you."

Then with one nod, off he went again, struggling with that candy wrapper.

Toil

Lovely, lovely day on July 10th, with the sun shining, but intermittently, through clouds bloated with white light. Glorious nimbi tumbling just out of reach like these marvelous living things, these luminous beings—jolly, intense, earnest beings—passing by on their way to wherever it is such creatures gather. I lay sprawled in my yard from six till noon, but no sign of Holzkind. I wasn't terribly surprised. His kind is a free spirit, untethered by appointments and obligations.

My yard was charming in its own way. It was overgrown, governed by the wild rather than man's hand, and the lawn was more like over-grazed pasture, but a manicure is not the only path to beauty. Nonetheless, it was not within the tradition of Cedar Hill to present one's yard in such a way. I had been meaning to take care of it for years, but as will happen, things kept getting in the way. Now, however, having taken an indefinite leave from medical practice and with Becky no longer around to occupy my time, it seemed an ideal opportunity.

In just three days' time I was able to turn all the beds, re-contouring some, dissolving others, even creating two new ones. At one point I made an exciting discovery as my spade hit stone, sending a rattle through the old posterior cranial fossa. With some careful digging, much of which was with my hands, I eventually uncovered an

S-shaped terra cotta tub that may have at one time been used as a fountain or fishpond. This, I knew immediately, would have to become fully functional once again.

Neighbors sometimes passed as I worked, pushing children or following dogs down the alley, and I would lean on my shovel, feeling the perspiration drip from my temple, and give them a smile, inviting them for a chat, but mostly they had other things to do. Ah, yes, I would remind myself, the scheduled life. I too was on that path not so long ago. Do not judge, Johnny, do not judge.

By the time the earth in the beds was turned and I had hauled in topsoil as black as a void, I was beginning to feel so tired that it was difficult for me to even get out of bed in the morning, much less push a wheelbarrow. But I had a vision that I could not let go unrealized and I was heartened thinking that most of the heavy labor was behind me. Now, I told myself, it was but a matter of sore knees and dirt beneath the fingernails. Or so I thought.

I never realized just how heavy potted plants could be. True, I had shed a few pounds in a short period of time, but my Lord, after moving but one fern from the Tahoe to the yard, I was ready to call it a day. And my cargo filled not only the Tahoe, but also a twenty-foot trailer that now blocked a good portion of the alley. Yes, it was rude of me to do that, but I knew that my indulgent neighbors would not begrudge me. They could just reverse their vehicles and go through the other end, which, by seven p.m., they had all done, some even with a smile. For the Magnusons, however, it wasn't quite so simple, as the trailer was also blocking their driveway, but Elaine Magnuson, with Matthew at the wheel, just rolled down her window and said to me, "Forget it, Johnny, we'll just park on the street for tonight."

"Many thanks, Elaine." I responded with a wave of my bandanna, my back bowing now from the weight of what must have been 500 pounds of dirt and flora over the course of eight hours of hauling. "And to you too, Matthew. Many, many thanks for understanding." Then up Elaine's window went, and down the alley they disappeared with a futuristic whir of the reverse gears on their new Honda Element.

By eight o'clock I had half-finished, and sat down in the middle of the yard, the dry grass poking through my dungarees, and had a bit of a rest. It was not my intent to fall asleep, but that I did, and was awoken by two little elves, Lars and Gustaf Van Pelt, one of them so close to my face that I was taking in his mouthy breath.

"Hello there, handsome boy," I said. This earned a wide smile, which admittedly was not hard to do. He turned to his brother, who had been making barefoot prints in the loose, rich topsoil, and without a spoken word, brought the other boy over to join us. Together they helped me to my feet, Lars (distinguished by a purple scar on his nostril from one of their countless outdoor adventures) on one hand, and Gustaf (distinguished by a deep, white scar on his chin from an entirely separate adventure) on the other hand. I was feeling light-headed; the yard swayed beneath my feet like a massive raft on ocean swells. All movement seemed delayed and distant; everything moving through a syrupy ambiance. The elves, with their mouths open like hatchlings, stared up at me expectantly, but for what I did not know.

"It's already dark out, gentlemen. Your parents must be very worried about you." Lars walked through the rusty gate and began hefting the plants from the trailer to the yard. Gustaf, not to be outdone, joined him at an accelerated pace. My first inclination, a result of my Minnesota rearing, was to stop them. I mustn't have these boys do my own work. It's not right. It's unfair. It's the pathetic act of a man with no work ethic. And then it occurred to me: Why? Why should I stop them? Was there any particular reason why the young men, so willing to help, so capable of helping, should be stopped from doing so? The answer was no. Mind you, some of these plants were literally the same height if not taller than the boys, but it was clear that the heavier the pot, the happier they were, as those were the plants they took care of first, competing against one another all the while. They had almost finished transporting all of the pots, a job that would have taken me into the next morning at least, when Peggy Van Pelt walked up to the fence with her arms folded across her chest.

"Good evening, Peggy," I said.

"Lars," she said, "Gustaf, please come with me." Then she began walking back up the alley toward their home. The boys looked to me, then to each other, and ran off after their mother.

Sweetie

Over a month went by and not a word from the dear wife. I had tried calling various places, friends and relatives, but never was able to reach her. They were able to tell me that she was fine and that I needn't worry about her, but never was I actually allowed to speak with Becky. And who could blame her, poor thing. Out of the blue, she's expected to deal with a sick mate. Unfair. Dreadfully unfair.

To understand Becky, one must first understand her upbringing, and to understand that, one must understand her parents, Carl and Sue Morganthaller who grew up in relative squalor in the Black Hills of South Dakota where Carl's father ran what was still called, back then, a trading post. Sue's mother was a schoolteacher and her father specialized in drinking and midnight beatings. Carl and Sue started their familial course early, as happened in those days, agreeing from the start that the objective in their union was to have children to whom they could provide all that is necessary in this world and then some so that they might know happiness and comfort, and moreover be shielded from the cruel side of life at all costs. A common tale, true, but what is perhaps overlooked in at least this particular case (although I suspect it's a bit more common than that) is that this objective, this matrimonial purpose, was not entirely benevolent. Carl and Sue wanted this because it simply was the object—the thing—that one strived for among peers. A child provided for was the equivalent of, say, an enormous house or vehicle, by the standards of my peers. And one of the tenets in providing for a child, in their minds, meant sheltering, shielding, and blocking all negative experience life might hurl at their poor children. And the more pure, the more unsullied and naive the child, the greater the parents' achievement.

To hear them talking, right in front of Becky, one might have thought they were insulting her. One of the first Thanksgivings we spent together, I was taken aback by what seemed to me the tag-team ridiculing of Becky between her mother and father. "Would you believe," Carl began as he carved the turkey, "our Rebecca, until her first year at Swarthmore, was under the impression that meat was merely shorn from farm animals as a sort of necessary byproduct, like wool from sheep, without any undo harm to the creatures?"

"Oh, and do you recall—speaking of animals," Sue quickly added, daubing cranberries onto our plates, "when she was in high school and sneaked off without our permission on a class trip to the Veteran's Day Parade, only to come home in tears, appalled that animal doctors should have so many missing limbs? Veterinarians, you see. She was getting 'veterinarians' confused with 'veterans.'"

"And the Torchlight Parade when she was a bit younger, with the large black fellow dressed up as a clown."

"Ah, yes," said Sue, her shoulders convulsing with laughter. "His face was only painted a bit, so she could see him for what he was. He wanted to talk to her, to ask her what animal she wanted him to make of the balloons, but she couldn't look at him. She'd never seen one, you see. A black, I mean, not a clown. She kept turning into my arms, fear in her eyes, whispering, 'His skin, his skin. What happened to him?'"

"Priceless," said Carl, himself now nearly in tears from laughter.

At this point, I nearly slammed my fist down, prepared to defend my sweet new bride. I had had enough and it was high time that these two learn that they would no longer be able to mistreat her this way. If Becky was intimidated by them, so be it, but I would not stand for it. Then, as I threw my napkin to the table, I glanced toward Becky and found that she was giggling. Yes, genuinely laughing along with her mother and father, enjoying their tales, and although feigning bashfulness, not feeling the slightest bit of shame as a result of their testimonies. It was then that I realized that Carl and Sue were not ridiculing their daughter for her stupidity, but in fact what they were doing was bragging. For, you see, such events in which their Rebecca exhibited her simplicity were evidence in their minds of the impeccable job they did raising the girl.

But what Carl and Sue did not seem to grasp is that we all, one way or the other, must eventually look the big black clown in the eye.

And so it was, on a swelteringly hot day in

mid-August, my brave-hearted little Becky ventured outdoors into the oppressive heat to pay me a visit, arriving *chez notre* around ten a.m.

She had let herself in, and began calling for me from the foyer. I quickly fixed what was left of my hair, splashed some cool water on my face, threw on a robe (the one of burgundy silk she had given me one cozy Christmas), and descended the stairs with arms open wide.

"Becks! Oh, sweetie, sweetie, sweetie," I shouted. Becky froze momentarily at the sight of me, then took a step backward and put her hands to her mouth and began to cry.

"No, no," I said. "I'm O.K. Just shed a few pounds is all. Looks worse than it is. Just woke up after all." As I approached her, she backed herself up against the wall beside the open front door.

"Oh, God, Johnny. I can't."

"You can't what, dearest? There's nothing for you *to* do."

"It's awful in here. It must be ninety degrees, Johnny. And the smell."

"Sorry, Becks, you're too right. It is a bit stuffy. Let's crack some of these windows shall we?"

"It's the height of summer. You've got to switch on the air."

"Alrighty then."

"I'm sorry. Can I just . . ."

"What is it? What do you need? Something to drink? Some air. Oh! Let's step out into the yard. I've got quite a surprise for you."

"No, Johnny, no. I just can't be here."

"Let's sit for a while. Have a little breakfast."

"I've already eaten. Look, I'm just not equipped for this sort of thing, and frankly I think you may have lost your mind."

"My mind? Why, my mind is a steel trap, dear. Nothing wrong there I can assure you. Right as rain. In fact, I seem more clear-minded every day."

"But this is what I'm talking about. You're demented. Delusional."

"Oh, come on now, Becks. No need for name-calling."

"Goodbye, Johnny. I'll check on you again soon."

"You're sweet. Thanks for stopping by." Then, as she was heading out the door, "Don't be a stranger."

Ojibwa Tea

Jean Kirkpatrick paid me a visit a few weeks after Becky stopped by. Jean, with her hemp clothes, sun hats and apple cheeks was the suitable misfit on Cedar Hill. Her husband was Dr. Kermit Kirkpatrick, Professor Emeritus of Agricultural Sciences at the University of Minnesota, but he was rarely seen in the neighborhood. Soon after tenure, Kermit made a sizable fortune by discovering a means of eradicating something called the shute bug for corn farmers. With money in-pocket, Kermit then married the prettiest graduate student he could find (Jean), and bought a home on Cedar Hill and a few hundred acres just north of Bemidji. Although we would sometimes see shiny new machinery that might come in handy on farmland, such as a luxury horse trailer with tinted windows or an industrial power-winch, it was well known throughout Cedar Hill that Kermit's land never grew a single crop or raised a single animal after purchase. It was the idea of farming that fascinated Dr. Kirkpatrick, not the act. Yet while other people laughed at him, I was always rooting for him. There was something in him that I recognized, and I wanted quite badly to see him finally transform those toys into tools. Jean, I believe, shared that sentiment, but also knew that her husband was not a man influenced by other people's sentiment. In the meantime, while waiting for

25

her husband to make his next contribution to society, Jean busied herself with noble causes and neighborhood functions, so it was logical that she would show up at my doorstep eventually. I would soon find out that it was in fact Becky who informed Jean of my condition and asked if she might check in on me. Just like that wife of mine, to aid me in my time of need and not even realize that she's doing it.

I was out in flowerbed Lana, named after my mother. The others were Bruce, for *mon père*; Cal, for my older brother whose last known residence was under a bridge in Honolulu; Ally, for my sister, a poet of some renown in Oregon; and finally a little spot for me just around the tub, which I decided would become a Koi pond.

The yard was a wide rectangle about twenty by thirty meters, one fifth of it separated from the rest by the path that wound down from the alley and garage (a structure situated a good distance away from the house and rather dilapidated for Cedar Hill standards). The remaining four-fifths of the yard was divided in half again, this time laterally. The farthest section was elevated and shored up by an unmortared sandstone wall. It was in that upper section that I had tidily laid out three of the five beds. Introducing the yard as one entered through the rusty gate was Lana, a bed of complex contours that would be filled with mottled blooms: purple zinnias, pink hibiscus, creamy plumeria, and golden euphorbia. A massive chromatic display boiling with blossoms, but capricious and fragile, especially with our winters. It was the largest of the beds and would lie fallow for much of the year, but when in bloom, it would radiate every gleeful hue divined by God.

Adjacent to and interlocking with Lana was the geometrically precise Bruce. Here a bed inexorably cornered by circumstance would provide vegetables and hardy greens. I would be able to harvest tomatoes, potatoes, and onions, and as the seasons cooled, the bed would blush with autumn fern and bubble with gourds and squash. Even through the dead of winter, creeping juniper would remain vibrant along the outer fringes of Bruce, using its gin scent and spiny foliage to ward off curious intruders who might be tempted to slip in beneath the iron fence along the alley or the tall cedar fence the Grobnichs put up for their privacy. And finally, assuring that Bruce would be distinct from the neighboring Lana, there would grow a dwarf winterberry holly, with its deceptively inviting berries and wounding leaves.

Nestling in the semi-circular arch created by Bruce and separated by a narrow footpath, sat Ally on a perfectly round knoll. Ally would be an herb garden filled with not only the requisite and piquant oregano, anise, and coriander; but also woodruff, becoming sweet when crushed; and hyssop, although sensitive during its initial growing phase could be robust when established, and eventually speckle Ally with blue flowers.

Stepping down from the stone wall, in the lower left corner of the rectangle, was my namesake—Johnny. Working with the pond as centerpiece, wispy fountain grass would soon bank its shores; a weeping Higan cherry tree, just four feet high and pruned like a bonsai, would drip downy flowers of pink and white into its waters. Lavender too, with lemon verbena would bathe the air, and honeysuckle would creep up the Grobnich's fence.

In addition to the cherry tree, there were already three other trees in the yard. A seventy year-old oak situated on the lower section shaded most of the yard, along with an uncharacteristically healthy birch that had grown into a V. The third tree was an elm, one of the few to survive the tragic Dutch elm disease epidemic of the sixties and seventies that nearly devastated the population in Minneapolis. Even Cedar Hill was under siege, yet our elm escaped unscathed. It stood tall and gnarly on the other side of the footpath just beside the bed named Cal. There I would add wild flowers and plants like speedwell, zebra grass, goat's beard and hay scented ferns. Throughout these unkempt reeds of green and white, Cal would be spotted with the royal purples of ragged robin, knapweed, and Russian sage. Yes, Cal would be unruly and wild, but at such a distance and severance from the rest of the beds, it would serve as an acceptable and amusing conversation piece.

As Jean Kirkpatrick wandered in, her eyes wide, I was putting in the tomato plants.

"Oh, Johnny," she gasped.

"Hello, Jean," I said, getting up slowly and dusting off my knees.

"Would you look at these plants!"

"Yes?"

"It's just that you don't often see these plants in outdoor gardens in Minnesota, do you?"

"Don't you?"

Jean, open-mouthed, smiled for several seconds then hurried forth with the reasons for her visit, saying, "Johnny, Becky says you're not well."

"Only temporary, Jean dear. Nothing to be too concerned about."

"Well, it's cancer though, isn't it, Johnny? I mean that's rather serious I should think."

"Nothing I can't conquer."

"Good for you, Johnny! Oh, God bless you and good, good, good for you."

"Thanks, Jean. Would you like something cool to drink?"

"No, thank you. You shouldn't bother."

"Not a bother."

"I just stopped by to give you a few things."

"Oh?"

Here Jean snapped open a canvas bag and came so close to me that our heads touched as we peered into the sack of gifts.

"What's this?" I asked.

"A remedy," she answered.

"Oh, that *is* good news."

"An herbal cocktail to rid your body of the toxins."

"Ah! More cocktails! Splendid!" I put my hands, dark with earth, to the sides of Jean's face and kissed her forehead. She giggled in return.

"We've got burdock root, sheep sorrel, slippery elm and turkey rhubarb."

"Marvelous, Jean, and what am I to do with it all?"

"Tea, Johnny. And I can show you how."

Inside, with the kitchen windows open wide to let in the *tierra mojada*, Jean rinsed, pulverized, diced and steeped until we had a rather nice tea. Each with a cup in our hands, we moved back out to the yard and sat on the ground.

"It's Ojibwa," said Jean of the tea.

"Ah, yes, Ojibwa."

"And thousands of people swear that this tea has cured them of their cancer."

"Fabulous."

"But the government and pharmaceutical companies will do anything in their power to keep people from having faith in a non-corporate cure for the world's biggest killer."

"Damn them."

"You know, you can grow all of these things here in your garden," she informed me.

"Is that right?"

"Yes, and some say that these particular herbs are even better in the colder climes because they're hardier and more potent for brewing."

"Fascinating."

"Isn't it though?"

"Yes."

We sipped our tea in silence for a while, and

when we'd finished I told Jean of my grand vision to transform the yard. She said nothing during this time, and eventually even stopped looking to where I pointed, turning her eyes instead to the ground.

"Is everything all right, Jean?"

"Yes, it's fine."

"Jean?"

"Yes?"

"Would you do me one last favor?"

"Of course, Johnny. Anything."

"When you see Becky, would you be kind enough to tell her that I miss her a great deal and ask if she might have just a few minutes to spare to stop by for another visit sometime soon?"

Unfortunately, my question had a bitter effect on poor Jean. Feeling such empathy for my pitiable state and apparently knowing more about Becky's situation than I, she began to sob. She could not be consoled and finally rushed through the rusty gate, tears still streaming down her face.

Contretemps

By fall, I had only managed to plant most of the vegetables in Bruce, adding at Jean's request broccoli and carrots, but my momentum was halted by a rather persistent discomfort around the sigmoid colon. At Inertis's insistence, I was scheduled to go under the knife on October 12, and on the ninth, an evening of cool breezes redolent with autumn leaves, I sat on the edge of my bed breathing heavily as I tried to ride out a bout of what felt like some sort of pointy-toothed creature at my bowels.

With the pain unrelenting, I was awake around 5 a.m. to hear the back gate squeak open then closed. Taking three deep breaths, I stood and went to the window, brushing the linen drapes aside. There, bathed in the most nascent of the day's light, standing with his feet wide and staring intently at the three beds of the upper level, was Holzkind.

Slowly—very slowly—I made my way downstairs and into the yard. By the time I arrived, he was at the dry pond, brushing some dirt from the stone. He turned at the sound of the screen door opening.

"Got sidetracked," he said. I was feeling rather too weary to speak, but did my best to smile as I put my hand out and moved toward him.

"This shit," he continued, "ain't going to grow

here, you know."

That, I'm afraid, is the last I remember, as I apparently passed out and went crashing to the ground. I awoke later that morning on my couch with a deviated septum and a black eye, but the pain in my small intestine had subsided significantly and the smell of breakfast was in the air. I shuffled to the kitchen to find Holzkind over the stove adeptly turning bacon, frying four eggs, and sipping coffee.

"Good morning," I said. He turned, spilling a bit of his coffee.

"There's plenty for both of us," he quickly said.

"Oh, good," I said but knew I would be unable to get such a meal down. Instead, while Holzkind ate, I prepared myself some of Jean's Ojibwa tea, which I had become quite fond of. He was finished and putting his dishes in the sink as I was pouring my first cup. At the sink, he stared out the window to the yard.

"What the hell are you doing out there?" Holzkind was not a neat man. His clothes hung from him like Spanish moss and his face was covered with filth and rusty hair, making his eyes—due in part to the pale blue color one might find in a sunlit glacial cave—seem immaculate.

"Tidying up the yard a bit."

"I'm pretty sure you don't know what the fuck you're doin'."

"Oh?"

Holzkind strolled out to the yard, picking his teeth. I followed. On his haunches, he pulled at the grass and rubbed dirt between his fingers. "What are you going to do with the lawn?" he asked.

"I was thinking a soft St. Augustine would be nice."

He turned his head to look up at me, squinting against the sun, but said nothing for several seconds.

"Would you mind if I had a seat?" I asked.

"I don't give a shit," was Holzkind's response. As I sat he stood, asking, "You got anything to drink in there?"

"Oh, yes, so sorry. Rude of me. In the Stickley armoire beside the Boesendorfer in the parlor."

"What?"

"Allow me."

"Siddown. I'll find it. How come you talk like that?"

"Like what?"

"Forget it," said Holzkind and made his way to the liquor cabinet, only to return not a minute later with the full Waterford carafe of Courvoisier.

"What happened to your wife?" Holzkind asked as he sat beside me.

"What happened to her?"

"Yeah, the blonde with the little ears that stick out. Nice legs. That one's your wife, ain't it?"

"Yes, it is, but nothing's happened to her. She's just staying with friends while I recoup."

"Recoup?"

"I'm a little under the weather at the moment."

"Under the weather. Looks like AIDS to me. Maybe cancer. That's some big time recoupin'."

With those words, I smiled, but was suddenly feeling exhausted. Hoping to turn the focus of the conversation, I asked, "You must have quite a repertoire of stories to tell living the kind of life you lead."

"I guess."

"If you wouldn't mind, I'm feeling rather weak just now and would love to just sit and listen to you talk a bit."

Holzkind agreed by launching into a tale that lasted into the late afternoon. Although born in Germany, he moved to the states with his mother and father when he was just a baby. They eventually settled in the mountains of Idaho. His father believed in living off the land, trapping and hunting. His mother was the one who understood commerce. Weaving, knitting, baking and sewing night and day, she would sell her wares monthly in the nearest town, five miles away. It was his mother, not his father, Holzkind claimed, that sustained the family and allowed them to live the life his father insisted upon. The mountains of Idaho, they quickly found, were deceptively bitter, and despite his father's great efforts, game was illusive to him.

Holzkind, however, took easily to living off the land. For him, reading the wild was instinctive. He could see things and sense things that were missed by his father. By the time Holzkind was twelve, he was a far more accomplished woodsmen. He could easily provide for the family. Then, in the winter of his fourteenth year, Holzkind awoke one morning to see the day was beginning with a heavy snowfall. So, Holzkind, already the man in charge, stoked and added wood to the fire so his mother and father would stay warm, and he set out to hike far into the mountains, checking traps and hunting deer. A full day's task, the young Holzkind was miles away when he saw the billowing cloud of smoke that would cause him to race back to his cabin home.

From miles away, the townsfolk, too, hurried to aid the Holzkinds, but arrived to find the boy, his eyes gleaming against the soot that covered him, huddled beside the bodies of his parents that he had hauled from the simmering home into a deep snowdrift that had now all but melted away from the contained heat within their charred corpses.

As Holzkind started in on a chapter involving a foster home, I realized that at some point I had gone from Ojibwa tea to Cognac. Wrong of me to be drinking the stuff, of course, but it was awfully nice to be sharing a cocktail again, and I believed it was the sort of thing expected of one in Holzkind's circles.

From the foster home (from which Holzkind ran away at the ripe old age of sixteen) he traveled the rails until he found himself in Montana. There he found gainful employment as a bartender and a young woman who loved him dearly, until pregnant, then hated him more than all her rage and violence could communicate. With the child miscarried and his life in Montana looking darker every day, Holzkind, at the age of eighteen, joined the army. This, as it would turn out, would be a step in the wrong direction, for it was there that he discovered the magical energy and inspiration found with cocaine, although this in itself was not what would ultimately result in Holzkind's dishonorable discharge at the age of twenty. Instead it was a little favor offered to a pal of his known to his comrades-in-arms as 'Dickless'. It seemed this young man with the unfortunate nickname was forever running out of steam before his peers. This inadequacy so troubled poor Dickless that he confided in Holzkind that he was going to have to quit the service, which he believed would result in his death either by his father's hand or his own hand. "If I can just make it through two more months I can ride a desk from there. No shame in that as far as I can see," the young man explained to Holzkind. And Holzkind believed he had the solution: methamphetamine, which he prescribed and supplied without a cent in return. Young Dickless died on an obstacle course the next day from a massive coronary.

Holzkind took a long drink then spoke unsentimentally, saying, "It's better some men keep to themselves."

***

His tale to this point had lasted several hours. Although the air was cool enough, we had been sitting in the sun for much of the day and the cognac was sending me adrift. My head swimming and my stomach sour, I was suddenly unpleasantly aware that what I had heard from my new friend thus far was merely prelude to the avalanche of narrative that was due to befall me. He had not even begun, after all, to talk of his life off the beaten path.

Then something happened that made it clear I would be unable to continue listening to his storytelling at that time.

"Oh, my." I said.

"What?"

"Well . . ."

"What?"

"It's rather embarrassing."

"For Christ's sake, spit it out."

"I seem to have shit myself."

"Oh," said Holzkind, pouring himself another.

"I can't tell you how very sorry I am. What a terrible host you must think I am."

"Yeah, well."

"I'm normally not like this."

"You better stop drinking that tea."

"I'm afraid I'm not sure what to do at this point. I hate to ask you to leave, but I'm going to have to go inside and when I do it's going to make an awful mess."

Holzkind stood, but something in his bearing told me that he was not getting up to leave. This was confirmed when, instead of exiting toward the back, he walked to the side of the house. He returned a moment later with the garden hose hissing impatiently, its flow stymied at the nozzle.

It was clear what Holzkind had in mind, and however obscene it might seem in hindsight (no pun intended), it struck me at that moment as the ideal solution to my mishap. Without a word exchanged, I disrobed, turned my backside to Holzkind and spread my limbs wide.

Now, while the Grobnichs had their eight-foot fence to block any unwanted view of this display, Mrs. Boerne (on the other side of the yard) from her second story bedroom window, had the opportunity for unobstructed observation. The poor woman was forever slamming her windows shut in an effort to communicate to the neighborhood her displeasure with certain noises—lawn mowers, leaf blowers, laughter, or children playing—but she kept an eye on us all. It sometimes seemed to me that no matter where I was relative to her house, I could look up and see Mrs. Boerne standing at her window as if there were in fact several Mrs. Boernes that kept sentry on Cedar Hill, but all of them tried to look as though she just happened to be standing beside the window, never actually looking out the window.

But the heartbreak of Mrs. Boerne's prying eyes is that she never had all that much to pry into from that vantage point. It must have been horribly frustrating to be prepared at every moment with an indignant gasp but never given the opportunity to deliver it. But as is the case with most sentries, their charge is a vista of ennui until that much anticipated call to arms finally arrives, and when it does, it arrives in spades.

By the time the authorities arrived, we were back inside and Holzkind convinced me, despite their determined rapping, not to answer the door. This seemed rather a simplistic solution to me. Surely, they would barge in with their battering rams and assault rifles, and seconds later I would be dragged from my home in shackles. And yet, not three minutes after their first knock, the officers got back in their vehicle and drove away.

Hospital

Although intoxicated when he said it, Holzkind had told me that he was an experienced driver, which led me to believe he would be able to handle the five mile drive through back streets to St. Edward's hospital, and ultimately the mission was indeed accomplished, but not before going through a rather hair-raising adventure. Speed bumps for example, were a new development to Holzkind. Crosswalks too, common around Cedar Hill Park, were ignored. In fact, the only time he did stop was for stoplights (not stop signs, mind you). At one point he spotted an acquaintance of his (well outside the parameters of Cedar Hill) and wanted to say hello. To do so, he simply put the Tahoe in park in the middle of the street and got out of the vehicle. None too happy were the drivers with whom we shared the road, as you can well imagine. Yet, Holzkind had no inhibitions about doing such things. When confronted on the matter by a heavy man of Hispanic ethnicity, Holzkind said, "I'm driving a dying man to the hospital. Show some consideration." The other man had nothing to say in return.

Holzkind was also due to pick me up after my requisite one day stay of post-surgery observations, but as will happen there were unforeseen circumstances. One being that Holzkind did not show up, the other having to do with medical complications.

The surgeon who performed my operation was a Pakistani fellow whose name I have never been able to remember. He was reputedly a master with the blade, but during a reception for an award ceremony we both attended some time ago, he had called me a "sycophant and a vacuous fuck." To my face. This, needless to say, left me ill at ease, not only prior to the surgery, but post-surgery as well. As I had no frame of reference for how I was supposed to feel after such an event, and my condition when I came to was one of absurd anguish, I couldn't help but consider that he may have done some creative tangling with my viscera. But not to worry, I was told, such sensations were to be expected. In addition to this pain, I also had a temperature of one hundred and four degrees that would not subside. Inertis seemed confident that it was viral, although I knew there was really no way for him to know such a thing without tests. With the chemotherapy sucking the life out of me, my body had little other fighting recourse than fever. It was the result of poisoning my body, and I was forced to pay the toll. Sleep of course was not an option, nor was eating, which after two days sent me into a delirium. Nothing prophetic resulted, unfortunately, just spinning walls and colorful lights. How long it lasted I do not know, but when it finally broke, I was down to a grotesque weight and a bit of my peripheral vision was diminished. I was, however, able to start eating again, albeit lightly; soup, Jell-O, Ensure, that sort of thing. Sleep, too, even befell me, rather than drug induced unconsciousness. Bowel movements, however unrewarding, were an event. Inertis was obsessed with my stool, although to use that term for the soupy excreta I was leaking into the pan was flattery. This was the ultimate goal of my stay at the hospital: eat, sleep, and BM. My raison d'être. If I could manage to fall asleep, then awake with an appetite, I was already on cloud nine. But then, if I could actually have a movement later that same day, well, that was the glory of glories, the holy trinity of St. Ed's. Not that it was a pleasant experience struggling off to the bathroom to perform the acrobatic feat of shitting into a pan without soiling my gown, then calling a pretty nurse in to collect it, but it was what filled my days.

On Halloween night the children from pediatric oncology stormed the halls with gleeful screams and giggles. Some had masks, others were dressed in scrubs, but none could disguise the results of this wretched fucking disease. One of the nurses was kind enough to give me a bag of candy so I could have something to pass out when the most courageous or jaded of the children ventured into my room. The kind of politeness from these children, I had never witnessed before. What, I wondered, made them so?

Around ten o'clock, as the laughter faded away, I was just searching for the remote to switch off the bothersome overhead light, when Spiderman came into my room. She was perhaps four feet tall, in a hospital gown and greeted me with a "Trick or Treat" muffled behind the plastic mask.

"Have you sneaked away when you're supposed to be back in bed?" I asked.

She adjusted her mask so that the eye-holes were better situated.

"Anyone in there?"

She nodded in the affirmative; her paper sack of treats rustling and her mask nudged again out of alignment.

"Good, as long as we're clear on that matter. But after this, you must go back to your ward because the nurses will be very worried about you."

Again the nod and she asked, "How much do you have?"

"Well," I said, caught a little off guard by such a blunt question after the others who had preceded her were so sweet and demure. This one, it seemed, was on her way to being a hold-up artist. Apparently she had been lying in wait until the others had run the circuit, so that she could then pass through to collect all the remainders. "How much I have, young lady is irrelevant, for you shall receive just as much as the others."

"No," she said pulling her mask down so the mouth hole was at her mouth. "I mean, how much longer do you have?"

Pirta

Mid-November I received a telephone call. It was not the first time the telephone rang, just the first time the call was for me and not a past resident of the room or the wrong connection. The call was from Holzkind, who was at my home calling from the line in my bedroom. I knew this because of the distinct crackle on the line that was familiar to me from calling Becky at night to tell her that I would be home late.

"They said you're still alive," he said.

"Yes, yes, I am."

"Yup."

"And how are you, Holzkind?"

"This yard's gonna get fucked up if you don't do something fast."

"Excuse me?"

"First freeze any day now."

"Ah, yes, I see what you mean. Any suggestions?"

"I dunno."

"Maybe you could finish it up for me."

"Hah! It'd take a half-dozen guys just to get the sod down in time. What the hell's the matter with you?"

"Could you get some people in there to do it?"

"I reckon, but all them tropical flowers and that faggoty grass you want ain't gonna cut it."

"There must be some way."

Silence on the line then, for some time.

"Holzkind?"

"You got some good money on this credit card here?"

"Yes."

Silence again, then, "I'll see what I can do."

It took me two days before I began to question the wisdom of granting a near stranger the use of my Amex Gold. It's just that I suppose I had felt we had been intimate in a way. Now, however, I began calling the house several times a day, only to get the machine whereupon I would leave shouting messages in the hope that H would hear them. "Holzkind! Are you there, sir! It's Johnny! Please pick up the receiver! I very much need to speak with you! It's immensely important! Regarding the credit card! Pick up the receiver! Holzkind!" But to no avail. Either he was not within earshot during my numerous calls, or he was just ignoring me. Or, perhaps even more likely, he had simply skipped town and was having a grand time at my expense, which I imagined was the sort of thing one did in his circles. There was a part of me that was actually heartened by the thought of H out there living it up, enjoying life as it should be lived. But as the days passed, I grew somber as I realized that this also meant that I would not see him again. Too ashamed of spending my money on himself without my permission, he would move on from me now. The idea of it, this tramp, this vagabond no longer in my life was suddenly crushing to me. It was so ludicrous, the fact that I was feeling lonesome for this man, it actually made me laugh, so loudly in fact, that it brought several nurses in to observe the behavior. Not knowing what to do about it, and seeing no harm in it as long as it didn't disturb the other patients (I know this was their thought process because they discussed the situation openly in front of me as I laughed), they simply shut the door and left me be.

It was at that point that I stopped eating. Not by choice, mind you. I simply couldn't stomach it. On day two of the fast I was put on a glucose IV and heart monitor, making any kind of trip off the island that was my bed a massive undertaking. Nonetheless, come Thanksgiving day, I demanded a wheelchair so that I could make my way through the decorative halls to the maternity ward, where I hoped the new additions to the world would brighten my spirits. It was in that way, IV bag sloshing overhead and my newly aged hands pushing against the wheels, that I rolled past the brown and orange crepe paper and turkey hands of construction paper. I greeted passersby with a smile and nod of my head, feeling suddenly like the host of this place where everyone else was either servant or guest. Except for the St. Ed's staff, the people when responding to my greetings, would either look quickly the other way, or glance at me from the corner of their eye and smile sheepishly, as if they weren't quite sure what the etiquette was in the situation. Anxious to extend these duties as host by welcoming the tots to the manor, I cut a corner tightly and nearly ran over good old Becks. I grabbed the wheels so firmly that I gave myself a burn, but Becky, in her graceful way, just jogged to her left and kept on her way, saying, "Pardon me."

"Becks!" I called as she turned the corner. A moment later, she peeked back around.

"Honey," I opened my arms to her.

"Johnny. Hello. It's good to see you." She gave me a peck on the cheek then knelt down at my side.

"It's so good of you to come. I know how hard it is for you to see me like this. But I'm happy to report that things are looking up. That Pakistani fellow—"

"Kashif."

"That's the one. And he's done a banner job cutting out all—"

"Listen," she took my hand in hers, "Johnny. I've come here to talk. To tell you something."

"Good, good. Would you like to come to my room?"

"No, I just want to say it. I'm going to ask for a divorce. I've moved on. I know it probably seems unjust to you, but really the way you treated me with this whole thing was rather inconsiderate. But frankly, that's beside the point. Donovan and I are in love and there's simply—"

"Donovan?"

"That's right."

"Wexler?"

"Yes, Johnny, and the fact that this comes as a surprise to you is indicative of your blindness to my feelings in this marriage."

"But what of Melissa?"

"She's with Alan Grobnich, now."

"What of Mrs. Grobnich?"

"With Ned Larsen."

"What of—"

"Johnny, please, I just wanted you to know, so that you could move on with your own life."

"My own life, Becks? You mean this sentence I'm serving here at St. Ed's?"

"God, Johnny, don't lose it here. We're in the middle of a public corridor for goodness sake."

"Too right, too right and I don't mean to be difficult, honestly, but perhaps we could just go over where I went wrong. To help me better understand."

"It's too late for that though, isn't it?"

"Is it?"

"Yes, Johnny. Yes, it is. I'm sorry, but it's over." Another peck on the cheek, a squeeze of my hand, then off she went, down the corridor, on her way out of my life.

"Oh, Becks!" I called after her as the automatic doors opened to her. But she didn't turn. "Happy Thanksgiving to you, dear."

No more sleep for me after that, and a moratorium was called on all travel off the island. Suffice to say I was not an image of life and vigor. My life was gone, my friends were gone, my wife was gone, my health was gone, and quite possibly a great deal of my money was gone. My yard, oh, my dear yard, that too would be gone by now. All the plants that I had brought in would have been killed by the several days and nights of freezing weather we'd had already. It was suddenly rather difficult to be a happy man, so instead, as I lay in bed hour after hour after hour, I turned to my memories. Those heady days of love and sex and hopes of even sweeter things to come, browsing the catalogues with Becky for wonderful things for our home, searching the glossy magazines for the perfect romantic getaway, strolling through the shops downtown for the ideal linen suit and picnic basket. And as the wind began to rattle at my hospital room window, I recalled those winters when the snow would fall so deep and dense that the children of Cedar Hill would literally tunnel their way through the park. And each year the neighborhood would rent a horse-drawn sleigh to pull us around the frozen lakes and through the city before the baffled stares of all those non-Cedar Hill folk. And after the sleigh ride, our noses and toes numb and pink, there was always a gathering at one of our gorgeous homes, often decorated well enough to make the December cover of *Better Homes & Gardens*. There we would sip our whiskeys and ciders, and stuff our cheeks with caviar as we warmed our backsides by the fire. Those were the days. And where had they gone?

Eventually the sound of the wind outside and these idyllic images floating through my mind lulled me gratefully into sleep; a lovely, deep sleep that seemed to last for ages. When I finally awoke, I could sense that it was the dead of night, and as I opened my eyes to the dim light, who should I find standing over me like St. Joseph? H of course. He wore my fur-collared parka and his beard was wet with melted snow. Breathing heavily, he said, "We gotta get you the hell outta here." Less than ten minutes later, I was on the heated leather seat of the Tahoe as Holzkind made his way back home. Although there was scarcely a soul out that night, H was driving much more cautiously than he had been on the way to St. Ed's. He didn't have much of a choice though, as the visibility was down to a matter of a few feet due to a cascading snowfall. The wind however had died down, which, despite the danger of the heavy snow made the storm seem gentle and even exquisite. The Tahoe's high ground clearance was still not enough to keep us from pushing snow at the nose. It was understood now when H didn't fully stop, for if he did, we would likely be unable to go again.

Cedar Hill, I could see from a distance, was blanketed in snow, but even at this late hour golden lights glowed from windows and smoke rose from chimneys as quaint as could be. But as we made our way up into the neighborhood, it became increasingly treacherous. Although Cedar Hill was usually first to be plowed by the city, there was no cause for the plows to be out that evening. With the snow falling so heavily, all efforts would have been quickly undone. Climbing up the hill, the snow gathering at our bow, the Tahoe roaring with effort, still could not finish her job. Just before the mouth of the alley, she gave out in a drift with snow up to my window.

"On foot from here," said H like Admiral Peary to Henson, then forced open his door, heaving it repeatedly until there was room to exit. Once through, he held out his hand to help me as I eased my way over and finally out of the vehicle. I had never in the past minded the cold during a snowfall, but with the meat gone from my bones it was bitter to me now. So much so, in fact that it was painful. Even with the parka that H had forfeited to me, I shook with rigors as we made our way up the alley, and my legs, atrophic and malnourished, ached more each second I was on my feet. Holzkind was quickly covered with snow, making his beard thick and white. He held me firmly beneath my arm, preventing me from slipping countless times on our ascent and lightening the load of my own paltry weight. As we trudged past the homes—the Goodys, the Goodmansons, the Whitlocks, the Princes—my eyes, shielded behind the fur-fringed hood, were drawn to their windows. During a great snowfall it is not uncommon for people to be kept awake with the youthful excitement that comes with it, and this snowfall seemed to have the entire corridor of the alley awake and at their windows, placing me, as it were, in the panorama of the gallery. Some had soft lights on inside, others were dimly lit by the luminous snow, but all it seemed were watching as H and I made our way up. Even children's faces were plastered up against frosty windowpanes, which—as I considered it—was not surprising, as every one of them surely prophesied the closing of their school.

By the time we made it nearly halfway to the house, it felt as though these eyes in the periphery were not so much my neighbors, but witnesses—no, spectators to what now seemed to be my Sisyphean struggle. I could not see how I would ever be able to finally make it to my destination. It simply seemed far too great a task with the convulsive shaking, the horrific pain in my legs, and the snow and ice collecting heavily upon me, my legs in particular encased in the stuff. But Holzkind was there for me, greatly supporting me on his side.

On the one hand, I was grateful to the man as he helped me along in this way, but on the other, I was angry with him for having taken me from my warm bed in the first place. As I considered this, I was forced to ask myself why I had agreed to leave with him. Why on earth hadn't I just stayed in my safe, private hospital room where I was finally finding sleep? Now, it was more than possible—cancer aside—it would be pneumonia that would hasten my demise.

As we reached the Tarkingtons' and Polks' I was heartened, for here I was finally able to see, however vaguely, the Grobnichs' tall fence standing like a black monolith in the distance. But as my pace quickened my footing became unsure and I was quickly down in the snow, my face buried in darkness and biting cold. Although only for an instant, there was this hush—an unearthly silence. People for whom snow is an alien thing perhaps don't realize the insulating effect it has, really unlike anything else, as its reach is vast and thorough. It can be quite a wonderful thing the way it will absorb sound, and with my head now enveloped in it and my body defeated, I constructed an inkling of the serenity of death. But the sensation was all too brief. Knowing that the faster we made it home, the better off I would be, Holzkind hefted me immediately to my feet, and I was moving again.

I moved deliberately now, concentrating on each footfall and finding that my burden was greatly eased. Suddenly, it felt like I was walking on air, as if I were not even crushing the snow beneath my feet. What the cause was, I did not know, but I was now more than able to carry myself through the storm. Except for my body's continued convulsions, the journey was nearly effortless. Even the pain in my legs was diminished. I looked down to witness the surge in the strength of my legs but what I found was that indeed my feet were breaking through only the very surface of the snow. That is, I was not reaching terra firma, only brushing through the downy corona of the building drifts. Only then did I finally realize that I was being carried. Holzkind supported my entire weight and had us nearly past the Grobnich's before I even knew it. I stopped moving my feet then, feeling mildly ridiculous for having been doing so for so long, and pulled back my hood to have a better look at this man. He was breathing heavily, steam pouring from his mouth and nose like a moose. His face and head were entirely white, with his two piercing eyes staring intently before him.

"Holzkind!" I said, and his breath halted for a moment with a grunt and he turned his head to me abruptly. I don't know why I called out his name, but he did not respond except to hitch me up on his hip like a mother with her tot then reach over with his far hand and pull my hood back over my head, never for a moment breaking his stride.

This, it occurred to me, is the sort of thing one does in his circles.

I began to sense it somehow before we even reached the yard. It may have been the fact that the Grobnich's fence was so heavily in silhouette, and I certainly must have begun to catch whiffs of life in this otherwise suffocated landscape. Nonetheless, as we passed the corner of the fence, nothing could have braced me for the shocking sight before me.

I have been accused on occasion of not thinking my plans through. Others, it would seem, have an ability to see when my ideas are overly grand or unrealistic. When I was in college, for instance, I made the decision to take some time off to become a rancher in Wyoming. My father, however, whose great wealth was earned in the pharmaceutical industry, could foresee that such a step would be antithetical to the fast-track plan I was on toward a medical career. Becky too, had the insight to reign in my unreasonable ambitions. Soon after we were married, I had purchased a 170-foot sloop, which I had hoped to renovate then sail from Nova Scotia to South America. Becky was able to clear my mind, pointing out that I didn't know the first thing about sailing, ship restoration, or—despite the cord of maps I purchased—reading nautical charts. But, when I came up with the idea to mend the yard, with my father entombed at Lakewood cemetery and Becks occupied with a mouthful of Donovan Wexler, there was no one around to point out the hurdles I would need to overcome. Fortunately, Holzkind was there to conquer them for me.

As we approached the gate, now trimmed with an intricate assembly of snow, the yard was awash with misty vapor and cleared almost entirely of snowfall. H set me down and I supported myself on the gate as I watched the snow drift down into the yard only to vanish away before it could hit the ground. Steam rose up from the brownish green lawn and the garden beds now covered with burlap rather than snow.

"Soil heaters," said H. "Keep moving."

I obeyed and we walked through the slushy mess to—at long last—my home.

Trap

Rather than make my way upstairs, I went to the living room where I fell immediately asleep. I was vaguely aware, over the next few hours, of Holzkind putting a quilt over me and then building a fire in the fireplace at my feet. The snapping of those damp logs was one of the most welcome sounds in my recollection. Holzkind too fell asleep in the deep chair with his feet on the ottoman and a throw over his knees. The poor man was surely nearly as exhausted as I. I felt as if for the rest of my life, however short that may be, I would be more than content to just stay on this sofa. If I never woke up again, that would be fine with me, and I realized—so profoundly that it seemed laughable that it was ever a question—why H was so determined to rescue me from St. Ed's.

Alas, at some pre-dawn hour, we were both startled awake by brutal and relentless pounding on the back door, a pounding so extreme that it shattered a glass pane in the door. Holzkind jumped to his feet and looked around the room, trying to separate his dream state from reality, and quickly made his way to the back door. From my new, entirely more blissful island, I listened as horror invaded.

There was at once shouting and some mild struggling, but hastily the commotion cooled and H returned to the living room with Peggy Van Pelt in tow. She was soaked in frost and red panic.

"Johnny! Oh, please, Johnny! I'm begging you. Pull it together for just a while. For just enough time to save him. Please, Johnny. The ambulances can't get through anywhere. It's madness! Johnny, please!" All of this delivered in sheer screams at the very top of her estimable lungs. I rose to my feet, a shock of needles running through my legs, and took her by the shoulders.

"What is it, Peggy?"

"Lars," she said.

When I was interning, there was much talk about the long hours of physicians. The concern being that the extended shifts were detrimental to their physical dexterity and cognitive reasoning. While this seemed a legitimate concern to me, I was struck by the outcry from the non-medical community. One hundred hour workweeks, in their eyes, seemed a ridiculous amount of work for anyone to endure. For many of these laymen, as I listened to and read their protests, they were in a state of disbelief. They simply couldn't fathom that we were working such interminable shifts. While I understood their concern, there was something I believe they could not quite grasp. While working long hours may be insufferable while picking apples or canning herring day in and day out, when we become stewards of another human being's life, we find there is a profound reserve that will carry us through. So profound, in fact, we will not even notice that it has yet been tapped. The drive to save or even aid another person is a tremendous and powerful thing.

Sitting in an old-fashioned toboggan that had decorated our garage wall since we first moved to Cedar Hill, I was towed by Holzkind, the sled's rope at his waist and little Gustaf pulling at his hand, both of them trudging and tripping through drifts. Peggy Van Pelt wandered off to the side, still utterly distraught. Considering the hard weather and the disastrous circumstance, the ride was oddly serene for me. Hidden by a thick wool blanket that happily engulfed me, there was even the hint of a smile. Until, that is, we reached the cusp of the railroad ravine. It was there that I spotted—before seeing Richard on his knees weeping helplessly, before even seeing Lars—the blood, the nearly satirical amount of blood that had spread through the snow, like iodine through gauze. I began to call out to H to tell him I would go on foot from there since going down the steep decline on the sled would prove too precarious, but before I could, he stopped, jumped over the towing rope and went crashing down the hill toward the boy and his father. Gustaf took me by the arm as I followed after with my medical bag heavy in my other arm.

As we waded toward him, churning up a frozen pink wake, I could now make out what Holzkind was so intently after. It seemed the poor boy, escaping with his twin from his mother's grasp to venture out into the newly white wilderness, had stepped into a steel-jawed trap just large enough to swallow his little foot whole and sink its teeth into his ankle just above the boot line. Although it was a simple enough device, Richard had not released the boy, likely because he had been unable to put all this in the right pockets of his mind—his delicate boy caught in an animal trap didn't compute for Richard, an actuary by profession. How does such a thing, this instrument of the wild, even arrive here on Cedar Hill, Richard must have been asking himself. But for Holzkind it was surely not curiosity that possessed him as he pried open the steel jaws, but rather sinking irrepressible guilt. The pain of it, those metal teeth sliding back out of his ankle and releasing his foot into a sad little hang, put the boy out and sent the blood flowing anew. Handing Gustaf off to his mother who buried his face into her hip, I dropped to my knees before Lars and removed his puffy Moon Boot. Both bones in the ankle, the distal tibia and fibula, were snapped, but an artery on the top of the foot called the dorsalis pedis was intact. It was the posterior tibial that was the source of so much blood, but having one of those two arteries still functioning was encouraging. With Lars in shock, I reset the ankle with little reaction from him, but a tremendous response from the gallery: Peggy howling and Richard retching. But to Richard's credit, he did not falter when called upon. I filled his hands with every 4-by-4 pad I had in my kit and guided him to Lars's ankle, wrapping his grip around the wound bidding him, "the tighter the better." Turning to Holzkind, I then pointed to the sled and said, "Pull a board and break it in two." He was at the task before I finished my sentence, but it proved to be more difficult than I had imagined. It seemed the toboggan was crafted at a time when workmanship and quality meant something. H pulled and pounded at the board, but could not for the life of him pry one loose. It was little Peggy Van Pelt, yanking the sled from H's hands and smashing it against the nearest oak, who ultimately handed me the boards I needed to fix the splint around the ankle. Thinking back now, I estimate all of this took perhaps just over one minute. It was the journey back that was most time consuming and trying. Not only because the passage was straining, but also because it was heavy on all of our minds, I believe, that even when we did get back, little Lars would still be in dire need of more complete medical attention. That is, the boy needed a hospital, but we had no idea how to get him there. It makes for an especially arduous journey when the destination is not victory, but rather another leg in which the route and degree of difficulty are unknown.

But lo: as we reached the alley, Dr. Kermit Kirkpatrick and Ojibwa Tea-Jean sat gallantly in their apple red F-350 extended cab pickup with a pristine, yellow, 84-inch shovel at the grill, exhaust gurgling from its aft and 355 horses corralled beneath its hood.

Remission

When looking back at the spring months of April to June, the time when I was in remission and the yard was beginning to show hints of the full glory it will one day exhibit, those days somehow telescoped into a very neat packet, independent in a way from the rest of my life; an atoll in the silly sea that is Johnny Gingham. Now, on a sultry Independence Day, the yard in a kind of primeval state, I grasp something that few people will ever fathom, good or bad. I am a dead man. That is, within a matter of days or maybe weeks, if I were to allow this disease to take its course, I will be dead.

The lawn has come out better than I could have ever imagined. It is like nothing else in Minneapolis, a fine coat in a nearly electric green. It is, I believe, the grass in the minds of poets when they think of a lawn. Other grass when seen from afar looks soft and inviting, but the closer one gets, the coarser it is revealed to be. This lawn, my lawn, becomes more inviting as one approaches and in fact feels precisely the way one would imagine it to feel. Now, as I walk naked through the yard, the massaging tickle of those downy blades on my feet is dizzying. The heat is heavy in this early evening, the sun beginning to set. My ferns love it, as does nearly all of Cal with its wild flowers and reedy grasses, as happy as a Cedar Hill wife in a mud bath. My only regret is that

H will never see it. Consumed with guilt for what he did to that child with his trap, he will never show his face on Cedar Hill again.

The air is filled with distant whistling bottle rockets and the smell of one hundred barbecues. Children race down on bicycles, their rubber tires thwapping against the cobblestones, their eyes widen in shock as they pass by my yard.

The Koi pond is complete, the water cool on my toes, but the fish at this point are no bigger than goldfish. I step into the pool and let the water cover my body. It is an amazing relief, nearly as powerful as the overdose of morphine I pumped into my arm just minutes ago. The yard is swaying again, but I know it is only in my mind because the water in the pond does not slosh out. I close my eyes for what seems a moment, and hear the rusty gate open, and when I open my eyes it is nearly dark. The boys, the twins, Lars and Gustaf Van Pelt, are running across the lawn. They are barefoot except for the metal brace on Lars's foot that will have to remain there for a few more months. He also has a metal cane that has now become more of a toy for him than an instrument of medicine. It is wrapped like a barbershop poll with red, white and blue crepe paper. They each brandish a sparkler, twirling them through the air with infinite joy.

Part Two: Oh, the Plans We Had

Pencils for Martin

It is bitterly cold out with two inches of snow on the ground, but Betty has made it in to open up the store. Just as she's putting in the till, the phone rings. It's Ginger Freundlich checking to make sure that Betty opens up on time, but she tries to make it sound as if she's just checking after Betty's well-being.

"I was worried that you'd break your neck on the walk in."

"Oh no. I'm fine. The shovelers have already come by. I'll be sure to salt out front, though, as soon as I've finished with the till."

"That's fine, Betty. That's just fine. As long as you're all right."

They say their goodbyes and Betty imagines Mrs. Freundlich hanging up the phone by her bedside and falling back asleep beside her husband Francis, whom Betty much prefers to deal with when it comes to business.

Today will be a trying day, Betty knows. At sixty years old, she would much rather spend the day waking up late and watching her stories. Perhaps meeting with her neighbor, Mrs. Kobeski, for lunch.

Knowing that the buses would be running late, Betty got up early to make sure she'd get in on time from northeast Minneapolis. There are those days when people are waiting at the door when she opens; today could have been one of those days. Someone needing hot chocolate or soup for what will be a long, cold day. The forecast said that the snow might come down heavy later in the morning and she knows there may be people who want to stock up on goodies so they don't have to venture out later.

After putting in the till, Betty shuffles to the back to retrieve a bag of salt. Just as she's picking up the bag, making sure not to throw out her back, the phone rings again. She picks up the pace back toward the counter, but as she gets there, the phone stops ringing.

As she dusts the front walk with salt, Betty smells the air and, contradicting the weatherman, forecasts a rise in temperature later in the day that will hold off any additional snowfall that might have been heading their way.

On her way back in the store, she drops the bag of salt beside the door and the phone rings yet again. She can't tell if it just started ringing or began as she dropped the bag. She moves as quickly as she can behind the counter and grabs the receiver.

"Freundlich's Corner Store."

"Oh, you *are* open," says the caller, a woman speaking quickly and breathing somewhat heavily. "Do you carry pencils?" No hello, no good morning, no how are you.

"Yes, we do."

"Excellent," says the caller and hangs up.

Betty takes the inventory clipboard from under

the counter and begins to make her way down the first aisle when the phone rings again. It rings seven times before she is able to answer it.

"Freundlich's Corner—"

"Are they number 2s?"

"Pardon me?"

"The pencils. Are they number 2 pencils? The kind of lead. Or graphite or whatever. Number 2 pencils."

"Uh," says Betty. "Yes. I believe so."

"You believe so?" asks the caller.

"Yes, we carry number 2 pencils."

The caller hangs up again. Betty makes her way back down the first aisle with her clipboard in hand.

Janice Goody has a thousand things to do today. Brandon, her husband, is once again out of town on business and she is left to run the home on her own. Martin and Kirstin, both at the same high school, are due to undergo some sort of in-school testing this day, but Kirstin claims she's not feeling well. Janice suspects she has been out drinking with her friends.

As she packs the children's lunches, Martin eats his cereal loudly behind her at the kitchen table. She finds this phase he's going through gross. She recently found a shocking amount of pornography on his computer; she worries that he could be one of those children who gets caught masturbating in a bathroom stall or peeping in the girls' locker room. Relative to his sister, however, Martin is a saint. The boys Kirstin associates with Janice wouldn't call children at all. They are big and look like criminals. What is more, it seems it is their objective to look like criminals. There is no pretense of actually introducing her friends to her mother anymore. They simply wander past her as if she were the hired help.

She stops packing the lunches to listen for any movement coming from upstairs, but there is none. Kirstin is still in bed. Janice shoves the lunches aside and marches upstairs calling, "Kirstin! Kirstin, it is already after seven." She pushes open Kirstin's bedroom door to find her hunched over the wastebasket—a wicker basket with no liner in it—heaving, everything curtained by her long brown hair. Janice gasps in frustration and rushes to the bathroom, drenches a hand towel in cold water and grabs another bath towel.

As Janice puts the wet towel to her neck, Kirstin breathes heavily with her face still buried behind the basket and hair, and Janice can smell the reek of peach schnapps.

"Was it worth it?" Janice asks, and Kirstin flings her head up, her hair snapping Janice in the face.

"Get the fuck away from me!"

Janice puts the dry towel across Kirstin's shoulder and says, "You're going to school today. Get ready."

"Can you not see that I'm sick? I'm not going anywhere!"

Janice stands and tosses the damp towel in Kirstin's lap and turns to go, but is startled to find Martin standing in the doorway, looking bored and sleepy.

"I need two number 2 pencils," says Martin.

The stool that Betty sits on as she stocks these lower shelves is narrower than her behind, and she uses it only when she is alone. She would not allow herself to be seen rolling over the edges of this seat. But it is not terribly uncomfortable until she stands, which she does presently with great effort.

On her way back to the counter, she catches a whiff of the secretion in the corner of the store. It has been there—off and on—for maybe two years now. She has been unable to make it stop, hide it, or find its source. The color of the discharge is a very faint yellow with a syrupy consistency. Although customers have not complained, she has noticed a foul odor from it, similar to the smell when her apartment building was exterminated and the mice decomposed between the walls.

She uses scalding hot water and a good deal of ammonia to clean it up. The store is clean. Always clean. She can pride herself on that. When Mr. Freundlich comes in he always compliments her on that, while Mrs. Freundlich gasps and waves her hand in front of her nose saying, "Goodness, Betty, it smells like a science experiment in here." Betty scrubs at the corner then stops and stares at the wall before her. She wonders what is behind that wall. The space next door has been many things over the ten years she has worked at Freundlich's, from flower shop to deli, but most of all it has remained vacant. The whole building is owned by the Freundlichs and they have spoken many times of expanding the store into that space, perhaps opening a small café, but Betty knows by now that it will never happen. They have no need to do such a thing. Their lives are settled. They have no ambitions but what to buy next. It's easier to collect rent.

Betty taps the wall, notes the hollow sound and taps again.

Even while her husband Louis was alive, Betty worked. They had money coming in in those days and planned for their retirement together with big dreams. Work was enjoyable because it was something that brought them closer to their dreams. But now. Now she does it because she's up against the wall. Because she has no choice. With no children, it will be the state that will have to take care of her when she is no longer able to do so herself.

The door chime rings and Betty, on all fours, gets up too quickly to avoid being seen in that position. She looks over the shelves, sees that it is Asad, the mail carrier, and begins to swoon. She catches herself against the wall. Asad comes toward her quickly asking, "You all right? You all right?"

Betty smiles, saying, "I'm fine," but she does not feel fine. She feels like she could very well topple over. Asad puts his arm around her.

"Let's get you to a seat."

Betty is comforted by Asad being there. He is strong and seems capable. As he eases her on to the tall stool behind the counter she says, "Really, Asad, I'm fine. I was just a little light headed there. Thank you."

"You sure?"

"I'm sure."

Asad slowly puts the day's mail on the counter, an assortment of coupon pages and sale announcements, along with a few invoices. He looks at her again. He's concerned.

"Asad."

"OK, OK. I just want to be sure."

"I'm fine. It's sweet of you to be concerned. Now go. Before people start complaining about their mail being late."

"Let 'em complain. They'll get their mail. I ain't missed a day since James fell off them monkey bars." He moves toward the door now.

"They're all well?"

He opens the door, letting the cold air take over the store.

"Well as can be expected." Asad points at the bag of salt by the door and gives Betty the thumbs up.

"Just for you," she says.

Asad laughs, harder than the comment warrants, but Betty appreciates the sound of his laughter nonetheless. The door closes slowly behind him.

Kirstin has locked herself in the bathroom. Martin is in the Sequoia waiting. With Kirstin throwing her tantrum they wouldn't be able to catch the bus on time, so Janice tells them she will drive them to school. On the way, they will pick up the pencils. The lunches are in the vehicle with Martin, and he's listening to one of his hellish CDs so loud she can hear the bass inside the house from the garage.

"Kirstin," she says leaning with her head up against the bathroom door. "If you don't respond, I am going to call the fire department and have them come up here and break this door down. For all I know you could be dying in there. So just respond so I know you're OK."

But there is no response. Janice takes a deep breath and starts pounding hard on the door. Immediately, during her pounding, Kirstin screams at the top of her lungs, "Fuck you!"

Janice steps back, defeated. She lowers her head then raises it again and stiffens saying, "I'm setting up an appointment with a therapist for you today," then walks downstairs, grabs her purse, and heads for the Sequoia.

Martin lowers the volume as she gets in the car, but she turns it off. She backs out of the garage quickly. Richard Van Pelt, walking his boys down to the bus stop through the alley, must step quickly out of the way of the enormous gold vehicle. Janice sees them only after she has pulled fully into the alley. Richard is holding their hands, one on each side. She puts down her window and says, "Sorry about that, Richard."

"Could have been worse," he says. He is not smiling.

Janice returns the affront by accelerating quickly down the hill, her tires slipping and catching as she goes down the freshly shoveled cobblestone alley.

"Yes, Mrs. Freundlich. I believe it could be very serious." Betty stands behind the counter with the receiver to her ear as she stares at the mysterious seepage coming from the corner. "Worth having a look at anyway."

"We've had it looked at before, haven't we, Betty?"

"Well, I believe we did, yes, a couple years ago. But I'm not so sure that man knew what he was doing."

Betty can hear Mrs. Freundlich cover the receiver on her end and mumble something to Mr. Freundlich. Then she comes back on and says, "You know, you've pointed that out to me several times in the past as well. Do you remember that, dear?"

"Of course, I do."

"Yes, well, it's just that I never really actually saw quite what you were talking about."

Janice Goody comes storming into the store and rushes down the first aisle. Her car, the size of a tractor, idles outside with her sullen boy inside.

"I see," says Betty. "Then it must just be my imagination."

Mrs. Freundlich says nothing in return.

Janice Goody approaches the counter in her puffy down coat. She is breathing hard and her thin hair is falling in her pink face. She crosses her arms in front of her.

"Does that mean," Betty says to Mrs. Freundlich,

"you'd rather I didn't call anyone to inspect this problem?"

"Excuse me," says Mrs. Goody.

"I don't see why, if even you are beginning to see that it's just your imagination."

"I'm in a hurry," says Mrs. Goody. "Could you please help me?"

"I see," says Betty.

"Fine then," says Mrs. Freundlich.

There is a long silent pause from both of them. Mrs. Goody says, "Please," and lowers her hands to the counter, leaning in toward Betty.

"Thank you, Mrs. Freundlich."

"I'll check on you later today, Betty, to see how you're doing."

Betty hangs up the phone and tries to smile at Mrs. Goody.

"Good morning."

"Yes," says Mrs. Goody. "I called earlier about the pencils."

"Oh, yes. That was you. They're right down the very first aisle there, all the way to the end."

"Yes, I know where they are. Or I know where they're supposed to be. But I don't see them there."

"Oh, well let's go have a look then."

Mrs. Goody is already down at the end of the first aisle scanning the area before Betty has even shuffled out from behind the counter.

"I know they're there," says Betty, raising her voice a bit so Mrs. Goody can hear her. "I saw them with my own eyes when I did my quick, little inventory this morning."

"Then I must be going blind," says Mrs. Goody.

"Oh, no," Betty laughs, "it's sometimes hard to see with so many other things staring you right in the face. I know that as well as anyone." She's almost down the aisle now. Mrs. Goody stands up straight, puts her hands on her hips and turns to Betty. "I'm sorry for that smell. I'm trying to take care of it this morning. I'm afraid something may have died in the space next door. If you look in that corner—"

"Would you please!"

Betty stares at Mrs. Goody for a moment, gains her composure and looks down at the small selection of pencils. "Let's see," she says. "There they are."

"Yes, I can see there are pencils there, but I specifically asked for number 2s. I do not see any number 2 pencils there."

"Oh, I see. Well, yes, those—ah, here we are. These pretty little ones say they're number 2s."

"No."

"Pardon me?" asks Betty.

"The heart pencils?"

"Yes, that's right. And these as well, here with the Teddy bears. Aren't they—?"

"They're for my son."

"Oh, well, let's see. Does he like Snoopy?"

"No, no, I don't believe he does like Snoopy, Ma'am. Do you have anything with hot young teens on it? Or perhaps oiled up lesbians?"

Betty slowly puts the pencils away.

"My God," Mrs. Goody continues. "Do you have the foggiest idea of what's happening in the world around you?"

Betty stands up straight to stretch her aching back then slaps Mrs. Goody across the face. The phone rings.

Janice Goody tries to speak, but cannot find the words. Slipping into shock, she begins to hyperventilate. As Betty walks off to answer the phone, Janice puts her face in her hands and cries.

Martin Goody enters. He scans the store and spots his mother as she backs up toward the little stool Betty uses for stocking. She sits.

Betty answers the phone after many rings. "Freundlich's Corner Store."

It's Mrs. Freundlich. "Hello, Betty. I just wanted to check on that Snack, Inc. invoice. Make sure it came in this morning."

Martin takes a few steps toward his mother.

"Let's see . . ." Betty looks through the mail. "Yes, yes, indeed. Here it is."

"And what is the balance?"

"Let's see." Betty tears open the envelope.

"The teachers usually have extras on test days," says young Martin, staring helplessly at his weeping mother.

Janice snorts, wipes her face with her hand, and then wipes her hands on her pants. She takes a deep breath. "Let's go," she says as she stands and walks out the door with Martin following her.

The door chimes and Betty calls after them, "Be careful on that snow now."

After dropping Martin at school, Janice returns home to find Kirstin back in bed. Janice sits at the kitchen table a moment gazing off into space. Her hair is a shambles, her face is puffy and she can actually feel how horrible she must look right now. She starts to cry a little, but it doesn't come the way she wants it too. She pounds her hand on the table.

It's quite a nice kitchen, with dark wooden trim and a warm ceramic tile on the floor. The window faces west and the deadened light outside is disagreeable to Janice. She grabs the phone and hits redial.

As the phone rings at the store, Betty is picking at the wall in the corner with a flathead screwdriver. She has set up a little work area, cordoned off by the caution sign she usually uses after she has mopped the floor.

With screwdriver in hand, Betty slowly makes her way back to the counter, the phone ringing relentlessly.

Behind the counter, she sets down the screwdriver and sits on her stool while she catches her breath. Finally, she answers the phone, "Freundlich's Corner Store."

There is silence on the other end for a time and then, "You do know that your phone is cordless, don't you?"

"Pardon me?" says Betty.

"The phone you are speaking into now does not have a cord. You don't have to keep it behind the counter. You can take it with you wherever you go in the store." Betty looks at the phone. Janice Goody continues. "So you don't have to haul your fat ass all the way back to the counter every time it rings."

Betty hangs up the phone. Flummoxed, she stays seated and slowly picks up the screwdriver. She smells the tip. It reeks like that wall. This will not do, she thinks, and looks around behind the counter. Her eyes rest on the ice chopper leaning up against the wall. She picks it up and chops it at the floor, testing it. The phone rings again. She picks it up. "Freundlich's Corner Store."

"You stupid cunt."

Betty hangs up the phone. She takes the ice chopper to the corner and slams the blade into the wall. In no time, she is able to create a hole large enough for her to see into. She leans the chopper against the wall and puts her hands to her knees. Struggling to catch her breath, she peers into the hole but can see nothing because it is too dark. Although cold air is falling like water through the hole in the wall, the heat in the store is getting a bit overwhelming. The smell of the heating coils burning, coupled with the salty odor coming from the wall turns her stomach. She glances back to the counter where she knows there is a flashlight. The distance seems challenging, but she straightens herself up and trudges in that direction.

Her eyes widen again as she stares at one of her handcrafted cabinets, hearing Kirstin walk across her room upstairs. It's a quarter after eight now. She would sleep until noon if Janice let her. What would she be doing out of bed now, she wonders? Janice puts the phone down and walks upstairs to her bedroom. Before dealing with her daughter—before doing anything—she needs a shower. She needs to be clean and smell like something pretty. She undresses, but finding herself exhausted she sits on the side of the bed. She considers calling her husband. But it would do no good. In fact, that call to Brandon could very well make matters worse, if possible. Janice hasn't been able to count on him for any sort of companionship since she can remember. Frankly, the man has become a dud. Even so, she picks up the phone by the bedside, but as she does so, she hears Kirstin's bedroom door open.

Janice, naked, rushes out in the hallway, still with the phone in her hand. "Where do you think you're going?"

Kirstin is horrified at the sight of her mother's shaking breasts. "Oh my God!" she says. "Get away from me, you freak." She turns her back on her mother and tries to slide past her, but Janice blocks her way.

"Tell me where you're going!"

Kirstin jerks her body to face her mother and opens her stance like an attack dog, her glittery purse swinging madly on her arm. "I'm going to school!" she screams, her face immediately a tremendous shade of red. Even her eyelids seem to fill with blood. The hatred coming from that little girl frightens Janice. She fears for her safety. And yet she is still struck by what an attractive girl she is. Her soft skin, her radiant hair. Such beauty in youth. What is it like, Janice tries to recall, to feel like a girl?

"How are you planning on getting there?" Janice asks as Kirstin pushes her way through.

Running down the stairs, Kirstin mutters, "A friend is picking me up." She is fighting tears, Janice notices.

"Who?" Janice asks, but Kirstin does not answer. She rushes out the door, slamming it behind her hard enough to rattle the windows.

Shining the light into the hole, it's still difficult for Betty to see, so she once again takes up the ice chopper and has a go at the wall. Now that there is a gap in the wall, it's quite easy to make it larger. Just as she removes a large chunk the door chimes. She turns to see the homeless man who haunts the neighborhood step inside. He stops there as the door closes behind him and stares at Betty. His red whiskers are frosted and his face his flush with the cold. He looks somewhat stunned, but that is the way he always looks, height of summer or dead of winter.

Knowing that he will be a while, taking advantage of the store's heat, she goes back to chopping. He will purchase a six-pack of beer and a candy bar. Perhaps some beef jerky, if he has the money. She has heard people refer to him as Holzkind.

Now she has the hole large enough for her to stick her head through. With the flashlight to the side of her head she looks inside the hole. There seems to be a bundle of some kind stuffed halfway up the wall. Perhaps the size of child. She shines her light down and sees another, and then just beside it, yet another.

The phone rings and Betty pulls her head out quickly, filling her curly hair with plaster and jostling her glasses with the flashlight. She turns, straightening her glasses, and is shocked to find Holzkind standing directly behind her. She lets out a gasp and covers her chest with her arms. Holzkind, calmly looks from the hole to Betty and back to the hole again.

Betty moves on toward the phone, ringing, ringing, as she shuffles through the aisle. She sweats now and wipes her dripping nose on a handkerchief she keeps tucked in her sleeve. Holzkind remains standing at the hole in the wall.

"Freundlich's Corner Store."

"How's business today, Betty?" asks Mr. Freundlich on the other end.

"Oh, hello, hello," says Betty, pleased to hear Mr. Freundlich's voice. "Pretty slow today. Everyone seems to be staying indoors this morning."

"Keeping busy?" he asks.

"Yes. Well, yes. May I ask what the status is of the space next door?"

"Vacant since June."

"Yes, I see. I wonder if something fishy is going

on over there."

"Why do you wonder that?" Mr. Freundlich is a somewhat dashing man, with a penchant for French-cuffs and an aftershave that smells of bergamot and orange peel. Betty finds him immensely handsome. He speaks with a cigar smoker's rough voice, but his tone is always calm and even.

Betty looks at the hole in the wall. "It's just that smell again is all."

"Betty," says Mr. Freundlich.

"Yes?"

"Let's let that whole business with the seeping wall go, shall we?" Betty dabs her forehead with her handkerchief. "It seems to be upsetting Mrs. Freundlich quite a bit for some reason."

"I see," says Betty.

"Can you do that for me, Betty? Just let that whole business go?"

Holzkind creeps up to the counter and places a six-pack of Highlife and pack of jerky on the counter.

"Yes, Mr. Freundlich," says Betty. "I can do that."

"Thank you. And don't you forget to call me if you need anything at all. All right?"

"All right." Betty hangs up the phone and rings up Holzkind's beer and jerky. Without a word, she places everything in a paper sack and Holzkind grabs it tight in his fist. The phone rings. Holzkind walks out the door.

"Freundlich's Corner Store."

"I could beat your fat ass if I wanted to." Betty does not hang up. She stares at Holzkind as he opens his sack just outside the door then struggles to open the jerky bag with his yellow teeth. "I'm younger than you are. I'm stronger than you are. There's nothing you could do to stop me."

Feeling herself about to cry, Janice hangs up the phone. She lies down on her bed and rolls herself up in the sheets and comforter. The whole bed crackles with a static charge. The sheets smell fresh, but she can smell her own body odor as well when the air whooshes up from the sheets and for some reason it makes her again want to cry. But she does not. She instead stares at the ceiling and thinks about how she can change her life. How she can get out of this place she's in. How she can be happy again. It's her fault, she tells herself, for letting people hurt her that way. They can sense her weakness. She must learn to make people fear her. She wonders, why do they think they can get away with hurting me? What is it about me that makes them want to hurt me?

Using a wire hanger, Betty tries to hook the bundle up above. When she snags it, it rips open and drips brown liquid. The odor strengthens. She gets the ice chopper, widens the hole even more then jabs it up to the bundle. It all comes tumbling down, garbage spilling everywhere. The smell is utterly overpowering. Betty gags and turns away. She covers her mouth and turns back to see the scattering of decomposing chicken bones, empty bags of beef jerky, rusty Highlife cans, and candy wrappers. There also, astonishingly, seems to be used toilet paper there as well.

The phone rings, and Betty rushes toward it, gasping heavily, and in just a matter of a few rings she manages to reach it. "Yes, yes!" she says. "Hello." The silence coming from the other end makes Betty want to scream. "What is it?" she pleads. "Goodness, what is happening here?"

"How could you do something like that?" asks Janice Goody. "How could you do that?"

Betty sits on her tall stool, catching her breath. She cranes her neck to see the gaping hole filled with trash then leans back against the wall, taking a deep breath. "I'm sorry," Betty says.

"What?"

"I said I'm sorry. I shouldn't have hit you."

Janice pauses for a moment. "I could have you fired. I could have you *arrested*."

"Perhaps."

"Is that why you're apologizing? You're afraid of the repercussions of what you've done?"

"No."

"Why would you do that to me?"

"I know who you are."

"Yes?"

"I know about your awful children. About your absent husband. About the volunteer work you do."

"Yes? Yes? Then why?"

"You know nothing about me. Nothing." There is

a crackling on the line. A hum of static. Betty listens to Mrs. Goody breathe through her mouth as if she has a cold or has been crying.

"You're insane," says Janice.

"Yes, sometimes, yes, I do think that. But not today." Betty hangs up the phone.

Mrs. Boerne comes through the door stomping her feet in her cute Sorels.

"Brr, Betty, Brr" she says hunching her collar up around her ears. "What can you do about this cold?"

"I believe warmer weather is on the way, Mrs. Boerne. All the snow will be gone by tomorrow."

"Oh, I'll kiss you if you can make that happen."

Betty takes out the black book that lists all the important phone numbers for the store. She flips through scanning for a contractor who can fix the wall and says, "A kiss would be nice."

Long Term Parking

Flying into the Minneapolis/St. Paul Airport, the woman sitting next to Brandon Goody put her hand on his knee. They were sitting in business class and had a pleasant enough conversation during the trip from St. Louis. She had had three whiskey sours during the trip. She seemed distracted or unhappy, but was not pouring her heart out to Brandon, for which he was grateful. Nonetheless, he expressed interest in her business and personal life. He was a good listener. She was attractive, though hardened in a way that made Brandon suspicious. Her nails, hair, makeup, and accoutrements were extravagant. She was a woman who spent a lot of time shopping, Brandon surmised. Overdone in a way that would have been unacceptable in his neighborhood of Cedar Hill. He was not from old money, but his wife Janice was and Brandon quickly learned how the nouveau riche were easily identifiable by the haste with which they spent their money in an effort to loudly advertise their new status. This woman was of that set.

Melissa was her name. She was the CFO for some sort of corporation that sold appliances and furnishings at discount rates to members, most of whom were developers. But now she had decided that she didn't want anything to do with it anymore. She was flying into Minnesota because she was from a small town in the

St. Croix Valley. Her family was there, and she was drawn to the area at this particular time in her life. Brandon concluded that she was at a crossroads and suggested that perhaps she felt the need to return to a simpler time. As he said it, he regretted its saccharine tone, but Melissa seemed touched by the idea and was quiet for several minutes afterward.

As they landed, with her hand on his knee, she said, "I would like it very much if you would come back to my hotel room with me."

This was not an ordinary occurrence for Brandon. Although not an unattractive man, he was boyish and tended to seem more fraternal to women than sexy. Nonetheless, he was not immune to seduction.

He stammered and glanced at his wedding ring. She slid her hand away.

"OK," she said. "I was just hoping for a little company this evening. I'm not a home-wrecker."

"No, no!" said Brandon, embarrassed for having implied that that was the case, although it was perfectly clear what she meant.

As they parted in the terminal, she said, "I'll be at the Hyatt downtown. Melissa Horner." They smiled at each other, and she added again, "I was just hoping for a little company." Then she turned and walked away. Brandon took out his cell phone and considered calling Janice.

He picked up his Saab at long-term parking. It

was cold in a hard and heavy way—eight o'clock and dark as midnight. Brittle flurries dropped under the white lights in the lot off in the distance and he could hear the crystalline tapping on the tarpaulin overhead. Brandon let the engine run for several minutes, warming up the inside, thawing the windshield a bit before he got out to scrape.

Downtown was quiet. A plow scraped Hennepin, its dirty yellow beacon turning sluggishly—a monotonous emergency. Janice would be on the phone now. Talking, talking, talking about nothing at all. Martin, his son, would be murdering by the score on some video game, or surfing the web for porn. God only knew where his daughter, Kirstin, would be.

He pulled up in front of the Hyatt. Just to think about it for a minute. Toy with the idea. People did it all the time. Did it feel as strange to those other people he wondered, as it did to him now? Did other people feel fear the way he did? As he was putting the car back into drive, the valet tapped on his window.

He knocked on the hotel room door and waited as she stared at him through the peephole. It was a sense he picked up as a young man when he was first starting in sales—an inkling that told him when someone was on the other side of the door deciding whether or not to open it. "Just here to introduce myself," he might say. Or,

"Just wanted to drop off some information for you."

Now he said nothing. Instead he pushed his thin hair off to the side knowing she would witness the gentle gesture of self-consciousness.

She opened the door in a forest green, silk robe with gold piping and a brocade crest at the lapel.

"Hello," she said. "Come in."

Brandon had not been in the suites at this Hyatt. He was interested to see that they had received the same upgrades as Chicago and Omaha. It was quite comfortable. The dense carpet matched Melissa's robe. The down comforter was stuffed invitingly high.

"Settling in?" Brandon asked as he closed the door behind him.

She smiled coyly, which did not suit her. She was not coy and the attempt at trying to appear as such made Brandon embarrassed for her. Her hair was coarse and perhaps might have been described generously on the bottle as honey or maple. She sat down at the foot of the bed. The television was on some sort of shopping network, at the moment pushing bejeweled dog collars.

"Help yourself to a drink," she said gesturing to the mini-bar, which was already open. Only now did he notice that she had a glass in her hand, likely another whisky sour.

Brandon poured a tiny bottle of scotch into a glass and took the chair across from her. It was leather and comfortable but considerably lower than the high bed. She had her legs up under her, a pedicured yet tough foot exposed.

"Did you call your wife?"

"Uh, no. No, not yet."

"Uh-huh."

Brandon finished off his drink and fixed himself another. While he was at the bar, she asked, "Will you tell me a little about your family?"

He turned to her with his eyes squinting, trying to read the tiny subtext.

"It's OK, if you don't want to," said Melissa. "I'm just curious."

"Have you been married?"

"No," she answered, and that was all.

"I have two children. Martin and Kirstin. They're both in high school. Martin is one year older. He is the product of an absent father. Kirstin, I'm fairly certain despises me. I don't much care for her either. She's a brat. But I suppose we're the ones who made her that way, so . . ."

"What does your wife do?"

"Takes care of the house. Raises the children. Volunteers a lot. Planting trees, picking up trash along the lakes, feeding the homeless. Her favorite pastime is talking on the phone. Hours and hours. She sometimes has two telephone conversations going at once: one on her cell and one on our landline. And then texting all the while. She's a real pro."

Melissa laughed, but Brandon could see that her eyes were getting tired.

"I'm sorry," he said.

Melissa shook her head. "Why do you have such

problems with your daughter?"

Brandon was confused. Could it be that this woman—this whorish woman—wanted only someone to talk to? Or perhaps this is the way this sort of thing always works. Maybe it was normal to have a little chitchat before hopping into bed. It made him slightly angry to think of how naïve he was.

"I can't remember when it turned, but it's been like that a good while. When she was just a tiny little thing, she couldn't say her own name. 'Kootsin,' she'd say. So we started calling her that. Particularly when she was blue or got hurt, we'd call her that and that had a way of cooling her down. But then at some point . . . You know what, it was in Florida. Have you been there?"

"I lived in Miami for two years."

"Well, then you know. We were in Orlando, but you know all about it I'm sure. How that place has this energy about it, like this carnival, suck-you-dry energy about it."

"I don't think it's the whole state."

"Well, anyway, all four of us were on the beach somewhere." Melissa scooted back, tossed the decorative pillows to the floor, and then lay back with a whoosh into the downy comforter. "Janice is good in that setting, I have to say," Brandon continued. "She was like this goddess. Something about the sun or ocean, but it brings out the best in her. On that beach I was looking at her tan—her T-shirt sleeves were rolled up over her shoulders—and the way her hair got lighter in the sun. The kids were wailing away, but she looked so peaceful.

Looking out at the water. There was a boat out there, the kind you can rent by the hour, but not for fishing. One of those luxury deals."

Melissa was smiling, but she started to close her eyes. It seemed clear she was about done with the chat, yet Brandon couldn't seem to stop himself.

"And it occurs to me then that we really need to get away from these kids. That sounds awful, maybe, but I just meant for a little while. Drop them somewhere so we could get on one of those boats. Just the two of us. Roll around in one of those pillowy cabins. And I'm wondering if Janice might be thinking the same thing the way she's looking out at that water. And just when I'm about to ask her, I catch a glimpse of Kirstin out of the corner of my eye. She is not a happy camper. She's looking at me like I've just gravely insulted her. Like maybe she knows just what I'm thinking, and how dare I. So I bend down and say, 'Hey, there, Kootsin, what seems to be the problem?' And she gives me a slap right across the face. Can you believe that? Four years old."

Melissa was still smiling. She gave a little guffaw.

"I should go," Brandon said. "You're tired."

She opened her eyes quickly and turned to him. "No, please." She opened her arms. "Please just lie with me here for a while." Her left leg was fully exposed now, all the way to her hip. Brandon took off his jacket. His tie. His shoes. Then finally lay down beside Melissa, holding her in his arms before him. She moaned.

"Nice," she said. "Oh." Then held his hand in both hers. His other hand rested on her hip. It was more comfortable than exciting, and he actually dozed off for just a few minutes. When he woke, he was aroused and began to stroke her hip. He pulled her robe open to feel her skin, which was remarkably smooth, and he guessed that she had recently waxed her legs. He put his lips to her neck hoping to wake her gently when there was an abrupt knock on the door. The kind of knock used by management or service people—definitive and loud.

"Ms. Horner!" a man shouted from the other side of the door. "Melissa Horner! Minneapolis Police Department. Please open the door."

"Um," said Brandon. "Melissa." She did not move. "Melissa." He slid his arm out from underneath her and put his hand on her shoulder. The lock on the door beeped and a young police officer entered with his gun held down at his side. An overweight couple, barefoot and dressed for the pool, walked slowly by then actually stopped for a moment to get a better look inside.

"Sir," said the officer. "Stand up and put your hands against the wall." He wasn't more than a kid. Hispanic, fresh-faced, and fit. "You too, Ms. Horner." He holstered his sidearm.

Brandon had his hands to the wall and the officer walked over to him; gave him the whole bit Brandon had heard countless times on television. As he was cuffing Brandon, the police officer's cell phone went off to the tune of a popular song he'd heard his daughter listening to. It was sung by a teenage girl, but the cell phone was a synthesized version of the song even more annoying than the original.

"Shit," said the cop. "Fuck," as he fumbled for the phone, dropping the cuffs, trying to keep a hand on Brandon. By the time he got the phone off, he was breathing heavily and it made Brandon nervous. He looked over to Melissa who still hadn't moved.

When the cop had Brandon in handcuffs he turned to Melissa and tried rouse her. When he couldn't, he called for medical assistance by talking into a radio at his shoulder. He then turned to Brandon and asked what drugs she'd been taking. It was only then that Brandon turned to the nightstand and saw the empty prescription bottle.

Brandon did not tell his wife of the incident, and she did not inquire as to why he came home a full day later than planned. For several more weeks, his life continued as it always had. Then one night after yet another business trip—this one to San Francisco—he came home and went right to bed. He did not wake for nearly 20 hours. When he did, it was late Saturday afternoon and the kids were off somewhere. From the bedroom, Brandon walked downstairs to the living room. There he sat beside his wife on the sofa. She was reading a novel, and Brandon placed his hand on her knee. What does one say to sell the most intimate proposition of all to the person with whom one should be most familiar? What's the angle? How subtle should the pitch be?

With his hand resting there a good while, she put her book down and looked at his hand then his face.

Thinking that there must be some sort of standard "rekindling" speech in his repertoire, Brandon searched his memory, but found nothing. He felt flush. He sighed. He looked at his wife, looked at the book on her lap, then—mustering it—back up into her eyes.

"Would you like," he asked, "to take a bath?" She looked at him sideways, accusingly or disgustedly or maybe just curiously, but remained silent. Brandon looked away and took his hand off her knee. "Forget it," he said. He ran through his options for how he could spend the evening. Maybe he'd get a drink downtown, or there might be some baseball on TV. Or he could just head back to bed. He felt as if he might be coming down with something.

"Give me half an hour," said Janice and she walked up stairs with her novel still in hand, her index finger marking her place. He did not move from his seat for 30 minutes. He sat patiently thinking about his wife and family. He considered his children and the lives they might forge for themselves. Was there still time for him to become a father? He thought about the impending sex he was going to have with his wife of eighteen years. He was a bit nervous at the prospect. Was there anything left between them? Then, emitted through the floorboards, came a precious squeak made by his wife's naked body shifting against the porcelain tub.

Her body was beautiful beneath the water, and with her light hair done up and her makeup removed she was more lovely than anything he thought he deserved in life. There was the faint scar just on the outside of her left breast, acquired hopping a fence about a year before Martin was born. They had sneaked into a public pool one hot summer night but got caught not two minutes after they dove in. When the lights in the pool house went on, they jumped out and Brandon hoisted Janice up the fence. But she was having a hell of a time. Not because she wasn't strong enough, but because she couldn't stop laughing. Even after she saw that she was bleeding, as they ran back to their little apartment, she couldn't stop laughing.

In the tub, Janice put out her hand to Brandon and he held it for a moment before he took off his clothes and joined her, both of them becoming a little giddy. They sat in the tub for a long while cleaning one another's bodies, saying little, until the water started to cool. Then Brandon climbed out and opened a towel for her, which she stepped into. He wrapped it around her with an embrace, holding her in his arms for a minute.

"Come on," she said. "Let's go to bed."

They made love, and it was sweet and enduring. When Brandon awoke several hours later, he was holding her in his arms. It was nine o'clock at night. The house was still quiet. Even the sound of rapid gunfire from Martin's games was missing. And the telephone, my god the goddamn telephone hadn't rung for hours. When he realized that Janice must have turned off the ringers on the phones, he damn near cried.

He gave her a light squeeze, but he had to use the bathroom and he was incredibly thirsty, so he reluctantly moved aside and covered her with the blanket.

After the bathroom, he put on a flannel robe and walked downstairs. He drank a full glass of orange juice quickly then stood there in the kitchen in a kind of daze, eyes open wide, like a shock victim. He felt a bit light-headed, and it was good. He felt at peace, which happened to him occasionally when he was by himself.

But then there was something not right. Something unsettling that he was trying to ignore, and did a good job of it for several seconds, before he could no longer deny that he was being watched. He turned his head to the window beside the breakfast table to see Melissa with her hands up to the sides of her face, peering through the glass. When their eyes met, she jumped back and Brandon's juice glass slipped from his hand, but he caught it before it went crashing to the travertine stone. At first retreating from the window, trembling, he then turned back and approached as if he didn't quite believe what he had just seen. He held his hands tightly to his chest, the way an old woman in a nightgown might do in such a situation. Indeed, Melissa was still there, now waving her hands before her, shaking her head, and mouthing the words, "I'm sorry, I'm sorry." Brandon shrugged. Melissa raised her eyebrows and pointed toward the front of the house.

As he opened the front door, Melissa was already there whispering, "I'm sorry, I'm sorry," as if she'd never stopped saying it. "I'm so sorry to bother you here at your home." Her hair was less busy than it had been, still colored, but softer; less handled. And her makeup was not as severe, making her eyes seem quite different; more innocent perhaps.

"I wasn't spying on you," she insisted. "I mean, not really. I would have just knocked on your door, but I didn't want to get your wife or kids. I don't want to put you in an awkward position." She looked past Brandon, checking the room. She wore a coat a bit heavier than a Minnesotan would wear for this spring weather, down filled and puffy with a small Saint Joseph medal on the collar.

Brandon seemed unable to speak for several seconds. He stammered, wanting to ask what she was doing there. He was a little frightened, maybe just an aftershock from seeing her through the window, or maybe because her presence unnerved him. Was she deranged, he wondered. It was an irrational act coming to his home like this. Did he have a lunatic on his hands? She looked a bit like one at the moment, and certainly sounded like one at the rate she was speaking. She had tried to commit suicide after all.

"I just wanted to find you so I could say thank you." She was on rapid fire, every word running into the next. "I wanted to have the opportunity, but honestly I didn't think I was going to go through with it because I'm so damned embarrassed about what I did, but then I got into town and just knew I had to. I've just got to let you know how grateful I am." It wasn't lunacy. Brandon could see from the way she tried so pitifully to look Brandon in the eye. She was simply mortified and desperate to reconcile her misdeed. "I tried calling, but the line was just busy forever. Oh, I'm so sorry too. I'm sorry I did that to you. It's awful, I know." There was a cheap, compact rental car idling at the curb. It was cold enough to see their breath as they spoke but Brandon was comfortable in his robe. It had rained a bit earlier and now the streets were shimmering and the smell of soil was in the air. It seemed every yard light on Cedar Hill glowed in the night. Mrs. Boerne from up the hill gave Brandon a nod as she passed by on her nightly rounds.

Brandon had found out later—a bit from the police and later from the papers—who she was and what she had done. She had been taking money from the corporation she worked for. Spending it on limousines, clothes, and home-improvements. Hundreds of thousands, if not millions, over the years. When she was finally confronted, she was indignant. Feigning great offense, she threatened to sue and then fled.

"I'm not on the run or anything," she explained to Brandon. "Just so you know. I was given permission to gather some things, make preparations with family before my sentencing."

"You seem content," he offered.

She brushed her hair back behind her ear, and looked down and away. "I took some pills before you got there. Then, at the door, I was so happy to see you. I didn't think you were going to show. You were so sweet on the flight, and I thought it would be nice if I weren't alone when I went. It would be really wonderful if just at the very end I could have someone."

A black Escalade pulled up behind the rental.

The windows were tinted, but Brandon knew Kirstin was inside, being dropped off by one of her boyfriends. Music thumped from inside, and no one was getting out.

"You're getting help?" he said.

"Yes. And thank you for checking on me while I was in the hospital. One of the nurses said a man was asking about me. I assume it was you."

"It was."

"You didn't have to do that. You didn't have to do any of it."

"Yes, well—"

"This is wrong. I'm sorry. I've made you uncomfortable. That's the last thing I want. I could have called or written you a letter, but I wanted to see your face." Brandon wondered if maybe Kirstin would witness this and see that there was more to her father than she had thought.

"How did you find me?"

"One of the cops. I told him I wouldn't tell." She laughed and shrugged.

"You've come a long way. You should come in."

"Absolutely not. I'm due back home." She gestured toward the car.

Relieved by her answer, Brandon nodded and glanced at the shiny SUV wondering absently how the boy driving it kept it so clean this time of year.

"It will be nice to be back home," she said.

"Good."

"You know, there's another reason I wanted to see you. I wanted to let you know that you've saved my life. I mean, you've changed it, I think, restored my faith in people again. I was dying blissfully that night, thanks to you. And now that I'm still alive I feel a little stronger." Her eyes were welling up and her pretty lower lip began to tremble. Brandon reached out and grabbed her shoulders, pulling her into an embrace. He closed his eyes as she cried on his shoulder.

After the embrace, she didn't say another word. She walked back to the car hugging her arms and sniffling. As she drove off, his eyes, moving with the grace of something pulled from distant density, swung back to the Escalade. He marveled at its cleanliness. It seemed to be the object of desire of every possible source of light only to be rebuked by its immaculate surface. He did not move from his stoop. He did not even consider it. The music got even louder, and Brandon watched, his shoulder cold from blue night air against the vestige of tears, as the vehicle carrying his daughter pulled away.

The Product

WEDNESDAY

It is revealed at school that your sister, Kirsten, made a video of herself dancing around topless in her room and posted it online. Praise Jesus that you did not come across it on your own. Miracle of miracles. Apparently she does not show her face, but took care to place things like the yearbook and some dude's letter jacket in the shot.

That afternoon, Lulu Tanenbaum, who is perfect and not in a bad way, makes eye contact with you. Lulu is already taking some college-level courses, but in the one class you actually do have with her, you can think of nothing else but how she plays with the top part of her ear as she listens intently to the teacher. She is the ideal human being and when you are near her—when she is even a passing thought—you feel like running. You feel so helpless and out of control of how the universe works that you need to run until you are so weak that you can't even think about anything ever again, much less Lulu Tanenbaum. And yet you know that if you could just be a part of her life somehow, even as a minor character, it would all be different. It would all make sense for you.

But the look she gives you today is one of sympathy. She feels sorry for you. She has heard about Kirsten and it is enough to make you want to go home and bury yourself in the backyard forever.

THURSDAY

Wallace, between first and second period, has some kind of fucking breakdown right in front of you when he drops his iPad in the restroom and the face shatters. He screams and cries hysterically like a little kid. Wallace is sent home and texts you to meet him there to play World of Warcraft and smoke some of his dad's pot.

When you arrive, the front door is open, but Wallace is nowhere to be found. The house is a massive monument of cement and steel. You always feel as if you're entering restricted territory when coming in past the heavy grey walls that separate it from the rest of the world. Even when you've been there for a while you have this underlying feeling like at any moment you might be pulled aside for a cavity search. After wandering the mansion's lonely cells and corridors, you finally find Wallace in the master bathroom where he grins at you as he pisses in a bottle of his mother's Bain de Soleil spray-on tan.

FRIDAY

Anwar Jalal backhands you across the face after school in the parking lot. Many witnesses, Kirsten among them, watch with glee and take out their phones prepared to capture the moment on video in case there is more to come. You look at Anwar wondering why, your eyes tearing from the strike, your face feeling like it's visibly swelling. You wait, thinking there will be some explanation from him. That he'll fill you in on why the slap was necessary. But there is none and that is explanation enough. He slaps you because you are alive; because your very existence is so contrary to the way he wants people to be in his world that it fills him with enough rage that he is forced to lash out in violence. Anwar gets in his immaculate black Escalade and roars away.

SATURDAY

You wake to your mom and dad arguing about the family spending more time together. "Kirsten is an emotional train wreck and Martin is a textbook product of an absentee father," she says. Dad reminds her, "He's your product too, lady."

In the evening you lock yourself in your room, plug in the headphones, and start scouring the Internet for some serious gamers.

This is your life. The very best you can do with your time on a Saturday evening is online gaming with your dad's credit card and a liter of Mountain Dew. And you're $120 in with no possibility of explaining this one away to the old man.

What's a guy to do? Run away and become one of those homeless kids downtown haunting the skyways? That would surely be better than the lecture you are going to have to endure from your parents. Or perhaps steal a good deal of money and leave the city altogether. Hell, leave the state. Maybe even the country. Does the Peace Corps accept minors?

But wait. What's this? A banner ad for a life-altering, game-changing, spiritually awakening organic supplement! 100% natural! Homeopathic! Herbal! Designed and formulated by Ayurvedic practitioners and holistic artisans! Guaranteed to change your life, balance your harmonic rhythms, and make you the kind of person you were meant to be! All this for just $19.99 and if it doesn't drastically improve your life IN EVERY WAY, you get your money back, guaranteed! Made in the USA!

Well, I mean really, you'd have to be an idiot not to at least try it. What do you have to lose? And besides, what's another 20 bones on Dad's Visa? Plus shipping and handling.

SUNDAY

You doze off early and now wake with a disgusting taste in your mouth. The computer is still on and it is still dark out and dead quiet. Not a sound in the house and not a sound from outside. The bothersome need to pee forces you out of bed. After the pee, you wander downstairs for water. The quiet draws you outside. The clouds are low and heavy with hints of red inside, and there's that feeling in the air like everything's close—like something might happen. You look down to see at your feet a red box about the size of those little milk cartons at school. There is no bow, no ribbon, no card or label. A warm gust of air blows quickly by and then it is still and quiet. You pick up the box and take off the top to find a tiny, amber bottle cradled in red tissue paper. There is a handwritten label on the bottle that reads only "Martin: One per day." Inside the corked bottle are five tiny pills. You glance up and down the abandoned street.

You sit on the edge of your bed staring at one of the little, white pills. After you put it on your tongue and it quickly dissolves, you tuck the little bottle under your mattress and lie back down on your bed. When you awake, it is nearly noon, and a yellow light shines through the blinds. Nothing has changed, you still have the acne, you are still a virgin, and you are still exhausted just thinking about life. And your room—good God—it's sickening. The stench and clutter is more than you can bear, in fact. You throw your sheets aside and begin gathering the trash thrown about your room.

It takes you all day, and by the time you've finished, you're a sweaty mess. You've removed more than what remains in the room, which is now immaculate. You have found a place for everything and cleaned every surface, pane of glass, and corner. The gratification it brings you is rather foreign, and you have earned yourself a long, hot shower, after which you sleep in a way that you don't remember ever having slept before.

MONDAY

You're up before the sun. Still no results from the pills. What are you expecting? Why do you keep taking them? You head down to the lake a few blocks away, and strip to your boxers. The beach still holds some of winter's cold and the water is fucking biting. And it is wonderful. You step into the lake and submerge yourself entirely; the soft sounds of the morning swallowed into the lake. You squeeze the muddy sand through your fingers and taste the iron in the water at the back of your throat. The water cools you behind your eyes and at the base of your neck. At first your heart races, and then, as you hold your breath and float through the darkness, everything vanishing away, everything becoming clear, the cadence of your heart slows to the rhythm of this watery adagio, a timpani playing sotto voce.

When you come up for air, you realize that from here you could swim through two lakes to get most of the way to school. Why has this never occurred to you before? You push off gliding across the still water and you are nearly done with the first small lake before you realize what a horrible idea this is. Nonetheless, you have already set out on this journey and you only need to skirt the northeast edge of the second lake to get to the road that will lead you to school. But as you pass through the channel, you realize that you may not make it. In fact, you count yourself lucky as you barely make it to shore. The walk is awkward, but not many people spot you.

It's still early enough so that not many people have arrived at the school and you manage to get inside undetected then hustle to the gym where you rifle through the lost and found box for some relatively clean clothes that will fit you. All you come up with is a Gophers football T-shirt and a pair of baby blue sweatpants that read "Juicy" across the ass. You also find a pair of flip-flops in the shower that will do the trick.

There is some taunting throughout the day, but it is surprisingly good-natured. Classes are tolerable today, and you can only conclude that there was some sort of conference in which the teachers were told to put more effort into their lessons so that they would be more entertaining to students. Everything is going rather well until the end of the day when Anwar trips you onto the asphalt and screams at you while you're down, "Stay the fuck out of my way, you fucking faggot!" Wallace watches from his Audi and waits to give you a ride home.

TUESDAY

In the afternoon there is a "Professional Development Seminar" in the school gym hosted by ViaTech Software Corporation. Anwar sits in front of you on the bleachers and the pocket of his letter jacket is pushed open in such a way that you are able to see the keys to his Escalade. As the ViaTech Team Hunters shoot T-shirts and caps from an air gun into the crowd of students, you quickly reach down and snatch the keys from Anwar's pocket.

In the backseat of the Escalade you find an Adidas cap and put it on low and tight, then you drive to the Déjà Vu strip club, but not before requesting directions from the OnStar navigation system and then running a camera-monitored traffic light. After spending some time in the parking lot of the strip club, you ask the navigation system the way to Planned Parenthood, then make the drive there, where you again sit for a few minutes contemplating just how Anwar is going to explain all of this away to his parents when they find out about the adventures their son went on this fine spring afternoon when he should have been learning the keys to success from ViaTech Corp.

You return the Escalade just as the seminar is letting out and drop the keys in front of Anwar's locker.

WEDNESDAY

This morning your dad tells you he'll give you a ride to school. Together as you walk down the front steps outside, you have this vivid recollection of the times you used to walk down the steps with him when you were a little boy. You recall a time when he was distracted and you took a spill and wound up needing six stitches in your chin. You don't remember your pain; you remember his pain because it overwhelmed everything else. You remember him holding you so close, his stubble against your cheek, his frantic breath in your ear, rushing, rushing, rushing you to the hospital. And you remember that after that he would always take your hand on those stairs. It was an automatic response for him after that. The two of you taking each other's hands as you took those stairs to go to school, to the park, to wherever. Always hand-in-hand. And now, as you head down those stairs, he's on his cell phone, but his other hand is out to his side a bit, fingers up and toward you, ready to take your hand should you need it. It stops you cold in your goddamn tracks, and when the old man turns back to see what's happened to you, you're sitting on the steps, the wind knocked out of you and a little teary-eyed. Teary-eyed, for god's sake.

THURSDAY

Anwar Jalal arrives on the bus. You arrive by water. Lulu Tanenbaum arrives on her bicycle. This girl is . . . If love is more powerful than what you feel for this girl, god help you should you ever fall in love. She is smiles and sun-reddened cheeks and shoulders. She is kindness and alert eyes; hair like the kind movie stars think they can buy. But they can't. She is the sweetest thing in your life and she is not even in your life. This must change today.

In the hallway full of those people, you walk up to her and you say, "Hey, Lulu."

Sarah On the Bus

Kirstin and Sarah stood outside Freundlich's store picking at their chipped fingernail polish and twisting their hair. It was fall and their extremities were cold. Kirstin, turned away casually to swipe snot away from her nose with the cuff of her jacket.

"This is fucking ridiculous," said Kirstin.

"I know!"

"We shouldn't be punished because of how old we are."

"I know!"

"Our money's the same as anyone else's."

"Seriously!"

Coming from a stroll along the lake, John Gingham, hunched and emaciated beneath a full-length down coat, turned the corner to stop by the store on the way home.

"Hi, excuse me!" said Kirstin.

John stopped suddenly, a little startled by the girls. He raised his chin and smiled.

"Hello!" said John.

"Hi," said Kirstin again. Although the blemishes in Kirstin's skin were minor she was tormented by them and covered her face with heavy foundation and makeup. The odor of perfume was also heavy upon her in an unsuccessful attempt to mask the smell of cigarette smoke on her clothes.

"Hello." he said again.

"We were just wondering," she continued. "Would you mind doing us a *huge* favor?"

John said nothing, but his smile remained as he looked back and forth between the girls. Finally breaking the silence he said, "You both seem so sad."

Sarah and Kirstin glanced at each other.

"Can you buy us a pack of Camels?" Sarah blurted out impatiently.

Sarah's plainness and weird sense of style drove Kirstin crazy. The bag she carried was the worst. A little turquois clutch she got at Ragstock. Something an old lady would carry at a cocktail party. Kirsten was forever trying to give Sarah a makeover—dye her hair, trim her ends, just a little makeup—but Sarah wouldn't have it.

"We'll give you an extra five dollars," Kirstin added.

John laughed then looked at Kirstin and stooped a bit to look her in the eye. He seemed to examine her face: the rouge, the heavy eyeliner, and the dangling earrings. Then her wardrobe: her too-thin jacket; her baggy, tattered jeans that flared over her Doc Martens; and her large handbag that looked like a chic Army satchel. "Aren't you Brandon Goody's daughter?" he asked.

Kirstin's mouth dropped open and she looked disgusted by the question. "No!" she lied.

They stared at each other for a few more

moments then John grinned and walked inside the store.

"God!" said Kirstin. "I hate this place!"

"Seriously!"

"Can't people just mind their own fucking business?"

"I know!"

Kirstin turned away in a huff and wiped her nose again on her sleeve.

"Let's just go to a store downtown," Kirstin suggested, then shouted at the front window of the store, "Where they won't be such *bitches*!"

Sarah added, "You just totally lost our business, lady!"

Jamming their hands into their coat pockets, they walked away toward the bus stop, slouching away from the cold.

There was hardly anyone else at Loring Park that day, but it was quite beautiful, with a handsome footbridge that spanned a pond stocked with Koi fish, and verdant willow trees with branches sipping at the water's edge and sheltering resting ducks and geese preparing for their flight south.

Sarah and Kirstin sat on a cold bench beside the pond smoking cigarettes and trying not to shiver. They were cold and slightly nauseous from the cigarettes, but they were enjoying themselves immensely.

"Let's just say he's not going to fuck with me again," said Kirstin trying to let the smoke drift from her mouth nonchalantly.

"Who does he think he is?" said Sarah.

"Seriously."

"Your parents pay good money for that school."

"I know. And he's all, 'I won't tolerate you wandering into class late so often, Kirstin.'"

Kirstin stomped out her cigarette and began rummaging through her massive purse for a piece of gum. A squirrel scurried down a tree toward the bench, and two others who had been impatiently monitoring Sarah and Kirstin, moved in closer. Kirstin found her piece of gum, folded it into her mouth and continued, "You'll tolerate whatever I tell you to tolerate, bitch."

"No doubt," Sarah agreed. "He works for you, not the other way around."

"Thank you."

Sarah and Kirstin bumped fists. Sarah flicked her cigarette away, and several squirrels rushed to investigate the butt. Quickly disappointed, they moved in closer as Sarah pulled from her turquoise clutch a small bag of miniature, caramel-covered rice cakes. The squirrels—nearly a dozen now—began to gather. When Sarah popped open the foil bag, two squirrels hopped up on the bench startling the girls.

"Oh my God," they said together. Foolishly, Sarah, already with a rice cake in her hand, threw it at one of the squirrels, but the animal snatched it in his mouth and fended off several competitors before retreating. Many more squirrels advanced to the girls' feet. Sarah and Kirstin began to panic.

"Oh my God!"

"Seriously!"

Sarah threw another rice cake down by the water in an attempt to make the squirrels chase it. Several did go after it, but more squirrels came in from across the park.

Kirstin giggled. "This is freaking me out."

"I know."

As Sarah put her hand in the snack bag again, a squirrel jumped on Kirstin's shoulder, causing her to scream and jump in the air, her hair whipping about wildly. Most of the squirrels dashed off to the periphery, but not all. Kirstin's scream also had the effect of startling Sarah who jerked the bag of rice cakes, spilling them all over the bench and ground. The squirrels swarmed, and several geese waddled over as well. Sarah and Kirstin ran away screaming.

On the city bus, traveling up Hennepin Ave, they sat quietly staring out the window, now feeling exhausted by the day. An elderly woman, fresh from the salon with her nails done in pink and her white hair in large curls, sat in a side-facing seat smiling as she watched the young girls. Sarah could see from the corner of her eye that the woman was watching them, but she ignored it. Kirstin, with her earbuds in and her cell phone in her hand, stared out the window, dreading the thought of going back to school the next day.

"Have you two been having a nice day?" asked the old woman. She had to shout to be heard over the loud roar of the bus.

Sarah turned to her, thought for a moment, and then nodded.

"That's nice," said the woman. "I'm glad."

Sarah smiled and turned forward. But the woman continued. "I've been enjoying myself as well. I've just come from the beauty parlor." She held out her manicured hand. "I know it's silly for an old woman to wear a color like this, but I couldn't resist."

"I like it," said Sarah. Kirstin slowly turned her head toward their conversation with a disgusted expression on her face.

"Thank you," said the woman. "Me too." She admired her hand a bit then asked, "What have you two been up to today?"

Kirstin went back to staring out the window.

"Nothing," said Sarah. "We went downtown. Then sat in the park for awhile."

"Perfect. I can't think of a better way to spend a Wednesday."

"I like your hair," Sarah offered.

"Oh, thank you. I get it done every Wednesday. Not my nails. I rarely have my nails done, but today I thought . . ." The old woman shrugged.

As the bus approached a stop not far from Sarah's and Kirstin's own stop, the woman began to stand up saying, "This is where I get off." Sarah watched her move carefully, awkwardly, being jostled by the movement of the bus. The old woman continued, "I need to start exiting now so I don't hold up the whole bus." Sarah smiled but averted her eyes, as if embarrassed or dismayed by the woman's frailty.

As the woman passed, she put her hand with its pink nails gently on Sarah's shoulder. It startled Sarah and she looked up quickly. The woman did not smile really. Nor did she say anything. She looked with her blue eyes at Sarah's face as the bus came to a stop, then made her way to the front exit, rather than the side, so she could say thank you and goodbye to the driver, and then she gingerly stepped off.

As the bus pulled away, Kirstin yelled, "Freak!" The other passengers, including Sarah, turned quickly to Kirstin who then burst out in laughter.

The bus driver's eyes in the rearview mirror continued to glance at Sarah and Kirstin, making Sarah uncomfortable, but having no effect on Kirstin who kept smiling as she thumbed through her phone.

When Sarah saw Kirstin's bag move on her lap, she wasn't so much startled as mystified. It just sort of shifted on its own, but not like its contents just shifted, rather like it had a life of its own. Like it was getting ready to transform into something altogether different from a gigantic purse. Sarah looked at Kirstin, but she didn't seem to notice or care that her purse was mutating. The purse moved again, more violently this time.

"Uh, Kirstin," said Sarah. Kirstin moved her head to the beat of a song, still staring out the window.

Again the bag jerked and continued to jerk until finally Kirstin looked down at the bag like it had just said something insulting. When the bag bumped into Kirstin's arm and continued to wriggle around in her lap, she threw her up hands. Sarah stood up just as a squirrel climbed out of the bag onto Kirstin's chest and looked her in the eye, its nose and tail twitching wildly. Kirstin froze for a long moment then finally let out a hysterical scream, stopping the bus and sending the squirrel hopping across the heads of the other passengers.

Kirstin jumped up and began high-stepping in place, flailing her arms and tossing her hair with her hands, presumably to shake loose any other squirrels who might be nesting there, all the while letting out little gasps of panic.

Other passengers began to panic as well, but as the squirrel made its way toward the front of the bus, the driver, as if this sort of thing happened frequently, opened the front door and the squirrel hopped off on Dupont, where it stopped to consider which way to go before deciding its destination was due west.

Days later, on a Sunday, as they walked through the mall, Sarah felt compelled to speak to Kirstin about the woman.

"What was with that woman on the bus the other day?"

"What woman?"

"The old woman you called a freak."

"Oh, my God. Yeah, was she like an old child molester or something? I wanted to slap her in the face. Why did you keep talking to her?"

"I didn't. God. She was the one talking to me."

"Well, you should have called the cops or something. She's probably off trying to rape some little girl right now."

"Gross."

Kirstin stopped in front of Abercrombie and Fitch to stare at a massive photo of boys and girls romping on a floating dock. They were all in bathing suits and had fantastic bodies as if molded out of plastic, and they glistened wet with lake water. They flaunted shockingly white teeth with their rapturous smiles.

"God," said Kirstin. "That is so what I want."

Sarah wondered if it was a body she was referring to, and if so, was it a boy's or a girl's. With her round belly and doughy face, Kirstin was far from either. But then Sarah understood that it was more than just a body that Kirstin was referring to.

They walked into the California Pizza Kitchen and Kirstin's cell phone rang. She answered it, "Hey," and then, "Nothing."

Sarah went to the restroom while Kirstin waited in line for a table, but when she opened the door there was a woman changing a baby on the little fold-down table, and everything about it made Sarah retreat. She quickly walked to Kirstin who was still on her phone and said, "Let's get out of here."

––––––––––––

In the SUV on the way home, with Kirstin's mom driving, Kirstin sat in the front seat with her ear buds in. Kirstin's mother spoke on the phone to another woman, explaining the jobs she had lined up for Kirstin the following year. She had spoken to some other people on Cedar Hill who thought they might be able to get her an internship of some kind.

"I did the same thing for Martin," said Kirstin's mom. Martin was Kirstin's older brother who was a junior at the same private school Kirstin and Sarah attended. "It's been good experience for his resume. I got him an internship at Jan Holtz's advertising firm during the summer. There were a couple of times when they were trying to push him around—you know, trying to give him too much work to do—and I had to make a phone call, but other than that it was great. You really need to consider something like that. They need to remain competitive. The market is saturated with kids like this. You need something that makes them stand out. Hang on. I've got a call coming in."

As they passed Cedar Hill Park, Sarah spotted the old woman from the bus walking with two other older people—a man and a woman. Sarah touched her knuckles to the tinted window.

––––––––––––

There was this feeling that overcame Sarah every once in a while. A feeling that seemed to be increasing in frequency. She felt like she was living in some sort of artificial environment. Like she was just part of a very long commercial for some unknown product or the parts of some reality TV show that were too boring to include in the show. She often wished she could change the channel or better yet turn it off—stop the show entirely so she could finally start seeing the world for what it truly was.

At school, there was a math teacher named Mr. Garret who had Cerebral Palsy. Since school began only a month ago, Sarah had noticed that he had gotten worse, his body bending to the side and his face contorting. She could see that he was giving up. On one particular day, he said nothing as the class began, and eventually students giggled, and realizing that he was not going to say anything they all found things to do on their own. Sarah watched Tanya Hart make a call on her cell phone and explain to someone what was happening in class, laughing about how weird it all was. Sarah wondered who Tanya could be talking to who wasn't also in class. Derek Bernaski took out his handheld and started playing games. Mr. Garret stared down at his desk, his eyes wide and watery; his twisted body slightly pulsing back and forth. To Sarah's right, two girls gasped at something they had just seen or read on one of their phones. Still staring at Mr. Garret, Sarah took a deep breath and he finally looked up; he stared right into her eyes. She did not look away.

Nor did he.

That day there was a pep rally toward the end of the school day. Kirstin and Sarah skipped out and went to catch a bus to the mall. While they waited, they had a smoke. It was significantly colder now, and they were desperate for the bus to arrive.

"Have you seen Anwar Jalal's Escalade?" asked Kirstin.

"No. He has his permit?"

"He has his license."

Sarah furrowed her eyebrows.

"He was held back a year," Kirstin explained.

"So, his parents bought him an Escalade?"

Kirstin shrugged. "I guess. Whatever. It's black and totally pimped out. He keeps IM'ing me and totally wants me. I'm tired of this bus bullshit."

"Here it is," said Sarah.

"About fucking time."

"Seriously."

The bus was suffocatingly warm. Although initially it came as a relief, it quickly felt like they were breathing through an old man's boot. Sarah pulled her jacket down over her shoulders and when she glanced at her, Kirstin looked green and stared off toward the front of the bus like she was trying not to move.

"Are you OK?" Sarah asked.

Kirstin vaguely shook her head, no. Sarah hit the bell strip, and when the bus stopped, they both gathered their things and slowly made their way out.

Once outside, Kirstin dropped her bag and as the bus pulled away she bent over with her hands to her knees and stared wide-eyed at her shoes. Sarah ran her hands through Kirstin's hair.

"I'm OK," Kirstin said. "I'm OK now." She slowly stood up straight. "God, that was sick."

"I know."

Kirstin took a deep breath of the cold air and as she let it go, the fog blowing from her mouth, she looked around and said, "Whoa, we're in like the ghetto."

They were not, in fact, in the ghetto, but had landed just outside one of the public high schools of the inner city.

"Isn't this where Jessica had to transfer?" Sarah asked.

Kirstin shrugged. "Let's go in."

"Seriously?"

"Yeah, I'm super curious," said Kirstin.

The halls of the school smelled of industrial cleaner but felt filthy and oppressive despite the absence of any trash and the windows that lined their way. Three other girls turned the corner ahead of them and approached, glaring at Sarah and Kirstin relentlessly. Two of the girls were black, one of whom was the size of an overweight man, the other a striking beauty. Such a beauty, in fact, that even from a distance it made Kirstin angry with jealousy. The third girl was white and thin in a sickly way, yet still carried herself in such a way that she seemed dangerous and rather frightening.

Kirstin stared back, but Sarah looked pointedly away, glancing through a passing window, and at cryptic, elegant graffiti made with fat, black marker.

As they got closer, the big girl stopped abruptly, taking a bold stance with her legs spread wide apart, one in front of the other as if readying to push a stalled car. She put her hands behind her hips, elbows pointed back, propelling her already ample chest forward. "You don't go here!" she said.

Without hesitation, Kirstin replied, "You know everyone in the school?"

"Maybe I do, but I don't gotta know everyone to know *you* don't go here." She wore a huge red, white, and blue Hilfiger sweat suit.

"What are you, like the hall monitor or something?"

The big girl stepped forward, the other two following behind. She got within a foot or so of Kirstin. "Girl, you better watch your mouth."

"You better tell your mom to cut back on the BGH milk before those things break your back." Kirstin gestured with her head toward the girl's chest. Sarah's eyes got wide and her mouth opened slightly. She wanted to say something; cut the tension—change the course of where this was all going—but before she could think of anything to say, the other girl slapped Kirstin across the face. Kirstin's eyes immediately began to tear, and the flesh where she was struck turned bright red. Sarah took a step back.

"Say something again," the girl said with supreme confidence. "Say something so I can slap that nasty tongue out your mouth." It amazed Sarah how in control of the situation the girl seemed to be. As if she had been through this sort of thing hundreds of times before. And Kirstin. Where did this courage come from? Why did she seem so willing to escalate this dangerous situation? Why wouldn't she just keep her mouth shut?

"Can I just say," Kirstin continued, "that Tommy Hilfiger better be paying you a shitload to be a walking billboard for him."

The girl took a swing at Kirstin again, but Kirstin moved out of the way and then lunged at the other girl and grabbed her hair.

The other two girls quickly pulled out their cell phones and began taking videos of the fight. They smiled and laughed excitedly. The big girl struggled to get Kirstin off of her, much of the time lifting her off the ground. Sarah, terrified at the prospect of winding up in a fight video online, rushed toward the other two girls, waving her clutch at them, trying to push their phones down and disrupt their shots. Together they shoved Sarah to the ground.

Finally, an adult came rushing around the corner. He was thick and bald and wearing a badge on his belt. He shouted as he ran. "Break it up, people! Break it up!" The girls took off running in different directions.

On the city bus taking them back to Cedar Hill, Kirstin and Sarah were quiet for a while, thinking over what had just happened. Then Sarah let out a small chuckle, and both of them glanced at each other and broke into laughter.

"What is wrong with you?" Sarah said through her laughter. "You're like some prison mama." This made Kirstin's face bright red, and soon it was wet with tears. "I'm surprised you didn't shank her." Kirstin was breathless, laughing with no sound.

As the bus came to a stop, several people got off and then a few more boarded. One of them was the old woman from the other day. Kirstin and Sarah slowly started to catch their breath. Sarah and the old woman's eyes met as she passed the reserved seats in front, and Sarah began to get nervous—concerned about what Kirstin would say to her.

She made her way to a seat just in front of them and sat down smiling at them. After she got herself situated, placing a large Marshall Fields bag between her feet and folding her arms tightly over her purse, she tried with some difficulty to turn toward them, saying, "Hello, you two." She only managed to turn about halfway, and so had to make eye contact through the corner of her eye.

"Hi," said Sarah.

"Another adventure today?" the woman asked.

Sarah shrugged.

"We just fucked up some bitches on the nordeast side," said Kirstin.

Sarah looked at her hands.

"You do not want to mess with us, Grandma," Kirstin added.

The old woman paused for a moment, straining to look at them, then turned back around. Kirstin nudged Sarah with her elbow and laughed.

After a moment the old woman turned to the passenger next to her, a man with headphones on, and touched his shoulder. He pulled off his headphone and she asked him to hit the bell for her, which he did without fuss and went quickly back to his headphones. The stop was not where she had gotten out before. It was several blocks too early.

The old woman stood, took two steps toward the front of the bus and stopped. She came back to Sarah and Kirstin. With her purse over her shoulder and her shopping bag in one hand, she used the other hand to hold onto the chair rail tightly. Sarah stared at the knuckles and taught skin, wondering at its strength and frailty.

She looked at Sarah and Kirstin not with anger. "I was once your age," she said.

The bus came to a stop.

"OK?" said Kirstin.

The old woman turned and continued on, passing the side exit, toward the front exit so she could thank the driver. Kirstin nudged Sarah again and laughed loudly. Several people turned to look at them, including the man in front of them with the headphones.

"Whatever," said Kirstin and put in her ear buds.

Sarah stood up and walked quickly to exit the bus.

––––––––––––––––––

Anwar Jalal's Escalade smelled of cherry-scented upholstery cleaner, sophisticated cologne suitable for an older man at an elegant affair, and spoiled fast food. He had not looked at Kirsten the entire evening. Not just avoiding eye contact, but literally not looking at any part of her. She asked him about school, his family, TV shows, but nothing would spark a conversation. His behavior that evening was contrary to the cocky persona he portrayed in his texts and when he was with his crew.

They had been at a party at Whitney Schooler's house and he flit between bursts of bravado when he was with his boys and bouts of what seemed like moping when left alone with Kirsten. He drank too much and she was miserable watching everyone else have such a wonderful time, and no one taking the time to try to talk to her.

She asked if they could leave after only an hour and he agreed without any sign of emotion either way.

She thought perhaps they could go for a drive or maybe stop somewhere to eat something, but Jalal drove her straight home. She found it embarrassing. Insulting maybe. Clearly she had been a disappointment. As they took the curve on the hill, she was confused to see that there was a car parked directly in front of her home.

"Hold up, hold up," she said. Jalal parked behind the other car. Her father was at the door talking to a strange woman. Still Jalal said nothing. She stared trying to make sense of what was going on. Was she a stranger who had just knocked on the door in the middle of the night? No, they seemed close.

She picked at her fingernail polish and looked over at Jalal. He glared like he was watching a video on the Internet, completely removed from the circumstance.

As she turned back to the scene at her front door, her father reached out and hugged the woman. "What the fuck?" Kirsten said. Jalal shifted in his seat as if she had just woken him up. The woman put her head on her father's shoulder. "Oh, my God."

They watched as she walked back to her car and drove off. Her father stayed at the door. What just happened, Kirsten wondered. What is going on? He just stood there, staring at Jalal's SUV like he was expecting them to get out. Waiting for them.

"Whatever," she said, then reached over and turned up the volume on the stereo and jammed herself back in the seat. Jalal took his cue and put the SUV back in drive.

At a stoplight somewhere just on the other side of the river, Jalal pulled out his phone and started to text. A car behind them honked after the light turned green, but he continued to text.

"Green," said Kirsten. He looked up and drove on. Only then did it occur to her that it wasn't her. He wasn't trying to send her signals. The problem, it dawned on her, was that Jalal was an idiot.

Red and blue lights began flashing in the mirrors and sirens where approaching behind them. Jalal made no effort to get out of the way. Several emergency vehicles passed them by but Jalal hardly seemed to notice.

Only as they approached the destination of all those emergency vehicles did Jalal show any sign of interest. He slowed to a stop in the middle of the street so he could get a good long stare.

It was fairly clear what had happened. A new tricked out Charger and a Ninja motorcycle had been playing chase and something caused them both to lose control. The motorcycle was banged up at the base of a tree. An EMT was talking to the dazed motorcyclist who was sitting on the curb.

The street was scorched with burnt rubber ending at a park where the Charger had jumped the curb and crashed into a stone bus stop bench, which had been broken in three pieces. Kirsten watched as they removed a body from the bench, and carted it off, covered from head to toe. From beside the broken bench, a police officer picked up a turquoise clutch and began looking inside for information.

A car honked behind them and another officer motioned for them to drive through. Jalal stared at the body as it was shoved into the ambulance. Kirsten stepped out of the SUV. He turned to her—finally—and watched her as she walked away from that immaculate shining machine and all the false promises it held.

Part Three: The Harpers

The Perfect Lives of Others

I am Shepherd Harper, son of Josef Harper the successful restaurateur, and Eloise Moore Harper, author of the popular *Tribune* column, "Tell Me Eloise" (formerly "Tell Me Moore"). There were six other Harper children—two before me, Graham and Martha, and four after, Walker, Antonia, Victor, and Lucy. Our home was at the top of Cedar Hill on Idyll drive. It was a nice home, large with classic lines and plenty of windows, but it seemed to always be in a mild state of disrepair. In those days of the early 1970s, we as a society were not yet so obsessed with acquiring the new or desperate for the pristine. Our storm windows and screens were ill-fitting and in even greater need of painting than the rest of the house. The concrete of our walkways and steps were crumbling in spots, with cracks so gaping that as small children we would hide things—army men, agates, Barbie shoes—in those crevices. When we would climb a ladder to retrieve a Frisbee or Nerf football we'd find the gutters filled with decomposing leaves and dead critters. The back lawn was patchy with dirt and weeds. But our house on the hill gave off a good smell, of a thousand thunderstorms, aching winters, and scorching summers stored deep within the wood. A smell of living fully and doggedly.

In the summers I worked the grounds crew at

Minikhada Country Club, a place seemingly unlike our home in every way. This was a world where every effort was made toward perfection. A world of rolling hills without an inelegant blade of grass or obstructive tree branch. Where trousers were pressed and mothers (of boys I knew) were fit and happy. I would work those grounds yearning to live in such a world, not be a part of the unseen efforts to make it so. On the eighteenth hole, in the earliest part of the misty morning, I would mow the green, my head filling with the smell of cut grass and gasoline; the grand, white clubhouse resting beyond the green knoll to the north; fog ebbing into the pine trees on the fairway; white sails gliding across Lake Calhoun far below. I would dream of perfect things like the homes of my friends, ads from glossy magazines, and a girl from the hill named Jenny Fitzmaurice with her wavy blond hair and Kristy McNichol smile. It was an entrancing setting and the often-methodical work I did lulled me into the world I wished for.

John Baumgartner broke my trance that day as he rode up on a blue tractor with his feathered hair flowing out from beneath a high seed cap.

"Someone took Victor," he said, and I pondered what those words could mean.

A week before my brother Victor was taken, a boy had climbed the side of our house to get to Lucy's bedroom, which she shared with Antonia on the third floor. It was not a particularly shocking event, as boys regularly made fools of themselves in an effort to gain the attention of Lucy, who at the age of sixteen was a striking beauty. But for Antonia it was horrifying.

We were awakened around 2 a.m. by the sound of Antonia's screams. My mother and father had only recently adopted Antonia from Guatemala, so her English was still poor, and she was not accustomed to what seemed even the most ordinary of things around her, making her seem a rather nervous kid to us all. We would find out later that she lived in morbid fear of kidnapping, partly because of a misunderstanding she had regarding the American hostages in Iran, and partly due to her past which would soon come back to haunt her.

Lucy was furious with our parents for bringing her into the family and took it as a personal insult to have to share her room with the poor girl. It is not too much to say that she hated Antonia and her fidgety manner, often complaining that Antonia kept her awake at night, crying incessantly into her pillow. A strange boy tapping at the dark window in the middle of the night put Antonia into a hysterical state, and none of Lucy's pleading would shut her up. By the time the rest of the house had arrived (Graham and Martha had moved out by then) the boy was already halfway back down the side of the house. Although there was enough light to see him, his identity was hidden by a bright green Edina baseball cap. Walker, Victor and I raced downstairs just in time to see him darting down the alley. We chased him halfway around Lake of the Isles before he jumped in the water and began swimming, his hat floating off in his wake. Victor, 13 years old at the time, tried to go after him, but we held him back—with great difficulty.

Victor's rage was fueled by two things. The first was a certain overprotective nature he had toward our family, particularly for the women, and of the women he was especially protective of Antonia who was just one year older than Victor. Although we all knew the boy was climbing the wall for Lucy, the fact that he had upset Antonia enraged Victor.

Victor and Antonia had grown close during her first months in our home. He picked up Spanish quickly by reading letters to her from home. I heard them occasionally, but could only make out that they seemed to be from a lovesick boy who demanded she return to Guatemala. Antonia saw Victor as her champion and he rose to the challenge.

But there was more to Victor's anger at that boy who climbed our wall, and it had to do with the boy's hat.

Edina—the place where the boy's hat proclaimed he belonged—was a suburb, a word like "sub par," "sub standard," or "substitute teacher" for those of us on Cedar Hill. It was an affluent place with no sidewalks and tacky houses with lawns that were rolled out. It was reviled for its artificiality and lack of character. We envisioned it as a place where Mom had dinner waiting when Dad came home from work, and there were plenty of Pringles and Chips Ahoy available for a quick snack. They drove into the city to use all our stuff, and then drove back to their ramblers with two-car garages jutting out in front and privacy fences in back. The kids were beautiful and athletic and impossible to take seriously. The colors of Edina High School were green and white, but the green was a special green that didn't exist in the natural world, somewhere between the color of new tennis balls and Astroturf. That's one thing Edina did right was pick that color green. In my mind, it perfectly represented a particular well-to-do country club style. The pretty moms at Minikhada had terrycloth hats that color, and some of their husbands had matching Polyester pants. Jenny Fitzmaurice had a tight-fitting T-shirt in that color, which read "I'm a Lover Not a Fighter." That color always triggered the craving I would get for that society of polished charm.

In the same way I was drawn to all idealized worlds, Edina too had a kind of allure for me. What would it be like, I would wonder, to come home after school to one of those split-levels and have Twinkies and a glass of milk waiting for me in the kitchen? What would it be like to go to school in the gleaming halls of Edina High School, where all the girls had shiny legs, teeth, nails and hair, like they were freshly unwrapped from cellophane; and the gymnasium smelled of varnish and paint. And yet, I hated Edina and what it stood for, a world with no soul and the retreat from reality. The paradox was this: we hated them because they were phonies but they didn't know they were phonies and therefore lived happy and content lives. It was maddening, and it was clear that Victor shared the same disdain for them that I did.

Although that event hardly seemed connected to this nonsense about Victor being taken, it is what first flashed to mind, likely because it was the latest example of Victor's difficulty controlling his temper, which, it occurred to me, could indeed be a connection. In fact, as it would turn out, the cause was much more sinister than a boy from the suburbs, yet it did find its roots in Victor's overzealous behavior.

When I got home from the golf course, the house was in an uproar. My mother, a woman who prided herself on poise and control, had Antonia's shoulders in her hands and had pulled her in just inches from her own tear-soaked face. She was pleading with her in the kitchen as Walker, Lucy and my father stood close by.

My father, wearing a dapper brown suit, looked at me.

"Have you seen Victor?" he asked.

"No."

He grabbed the phone from the wall and dialed zero. It was unheard of to see my father home during the day and as I watched him ask for the police from the operator, I noticed too that his tie was loose and crooked, something I had never before seen in my life. It disturbed me so much that I nearly broke down in tears.

"What kind of car was he driving?" my mother asked, but Antonia only shook her head sadly, not understanding. "El auto de tu amigo? Azul? Roja? Grande? Chico?"

"No se. No se. Una troca." Then Antonia collapsed to her knees, sobbing into her hands.

As we would eventually piece together, the boy who had been sending Antonia letters from Guatemala had come for her. While we waited for the police to arrive, we sat in our living room and listened to Antonia explain to us in English and Spanish that at the age of thirteen she had taken a lover named Abraham, many years her senior. Lucy's mouth opened slightly as she listened to Antonia's story. She actually moved in closer to her on the couch so she could put her hand on her knee.

This man, Abraham, as it would turn out, had been pleading with Antonia to come back, and warned her that if she didn't come back to marry him, he would come get her.

When he showed up at our home, Victor answered the door, and as their voices rose, Antonia heard them and came running downstairs, knowing immediately that it was her former lover carrying out on his promise. When Abraham saw her, he barged through the doorway, knocking Victor down. He tried to take Antonia in his arms, but she resisted and screamed at him to leave the house immediately, telling him that she didn't love him, at which point Victor jumped on Abraham's back and pulled him to the ground. They wrestled for a moment, but little Victor was no match for Abraham. Walker yelled down from upstairs over the railing saying that he had called the police and they were on the way. Antonia translated and added that they would show him no mercy here in the United States and he would be lucky if they only tortured him and left him in a cell to rot for the rest of his life. Although Walker had not actually called the police, a fire truck went by down the road and it spooked Abraham, sending him running to his truck.

Lucy put her hand to her gaping mouth and I could see the slightest bit of a smile around her eyes.

"How did Victor get in the truck?" my father asked.

"Victor run after him. He jump in troca."

"He what?" said my mother and father.

"In truck," she repeated pointing behind her then opening her hands in front of her in a gesture meant to communicate the bed of the truck.

Then, just before the police finally arrived, Antonia said, "Abraham es bad. Abraham es muy angry man." Then she patted her hip and said, "Knife."

That night my mother and father took the car out searching, while Walker and I searched the streets on bicycle. Antonia and Lucy were to wait by the phone and all of us were to check back on the hour.

By seven o'clock, there was not a single resident of the hill who was not assisting in the search. Mrs. Boerne, renowned as a snoop and a gossip on the hill, not only led the brigade, but as people arrived home from work and came out after dinner, it was she they naturally gravitated toward. I watched them—the Doremeisters, the Wexlers, the Fitzmaurices—come out looking up and down the street, shrugging their shoulders and when spotting Mrs. Boerne rushing to her for direction. I watched as Mrs. Boerne unflinchingly told them what to do and where to go, and what's more, I watched them all, without hesitation, obey.

In the morning, as I lay awake in bed, I debated whether or not to go in to work, finally deciding that if I were to stay home, I would lose my mind, but if I were to go to work I would only attract too much unwanted attention. As an alternative, I biked over to a friend's house who lived on Cedar Lake and borrowed their canoe just as the sun was beginning to rise.

The horizon was orange and lit up the lake. I breathed in the piney air and cut the plane of amber light. Tranquility seeps through the Minnesota mud and stone to form her lakes. Sending a canoe gliding across those waters, breathing the air that rises from them, is unequalled. It is life as it was meant to be, and what is more, it is unforgettable. The same peace that makes our lakes, courses through a Minnesotan's veins, and is gratefully innate. As I sat floating on that steaming water, the sun beginning to warm me, I thought about Victor and what could have become of him. What life would be without him. The loss of fire. It occurred to me that my desires and envy for those things other people seemed to hold out of my reach were a delicious distraction. And that desire was somehow missing now. My mind no longer drifted to Tony Delucci's Audi, or Reed Ashbury's Atari system, or the wet bar stocked with Fresca in Tonya Carlson's basement game room. Instead, I wondered if I would ever want again, and it confounded me because it seemed to me that it might be wonderful—to be empty and without—to be at a loss.

That afternoon, our father found Victor behind the brick water tower on Mount Curve, his face bloody, his hands bruised and swollen. We could not distinguish between the black dirt and dark blood that coated him. EMS found no pulse upon their arrival.

Within minutes neighbors gathered in the area. It was Mrs. Boerne who tended to the crowd, physically pushing people back, telling them to make room for our family. There was a doctor there, doing what he could before EMS arrived. We stood by watching the spectacle. Antonia could not be consoled. She sobbed in our mother's arms. Walker wept quietly, trying to fight the tears, shaking at a high frequency. It was difficult to read Lucy. She seemed baffled. She lived for sensational things, but this moment she was unable to categorize, perhaps feeling as though she had just fallen into an after school special.

As EMS took him away, into the truck, down the road, out of my sight, my eyes landed on the Yuworski's house and I thought about Debbie Yuworski, one year younger than me, who that year won a Ford Mustang from a Coca-Cola can, and I wondered where the Yuworskis were going to find room for it, as the Mustang would now be their fourth vehicle.

Someone gently touched my hair and I flinched. It was Mrs. Fitzmaurice and standing beside her was Jenny and her father. Jenny looked much younger standing there with her mother and father. I was about Victor's age when I first saw Jenny Fitzmaurice and felt something like love. It was spring. I was taking my skateboard down the hill. There were still brown crusts of ice over the gutters along the street, coated with grit, water trickling beneath them. On the way up the hill, I'd stomp on those icy shelves, listening to the hollow crack. Going down was hairy because the streets were still sandy and wet, but the sun was out and the temperature was above forty. I had already gone down quite a few times and was winded in an exhilarated way, high off all the fresh air coming from the new buds and soft green spreading across the landscape. My cheeks cool and the wind through my hair, I stood at the top of the hill ready for another trip down and spotted Jenny Fitzmaurice coming back from Freundlich's store on the corner. She was with a small group of kids and they each carried a small brown bag of treats of their own. Jenny was drinking a Tahitian Treat and the other kids were listening to something she was saying. They all laughed through wide-open candied lips and fog puffed from their mouths. I could almost smell the sweetness of their breath, even as I recalled it. I remember looking down at her and being struck by something about her. Although I didn't have the word to put to it then, the thing about Jenny Fitzmaurice that struck me was that she had style. The way she dressed, the way she carried herself, the way she laughed and talked, everything about her had style, even as a girl. It was a thing I obsessed about for a long time after that because I could see immediately that it was something she didn't try to do. It was something that was in her; a thing that she emanated. It was the thing, I would eventually come to realize, that Edina wanted so badly, but could never have. Because the more you try to have it, the less you do. It's the reason we all loved Jenny Fitzmaurice so much. She reminded us that there was no imitating style. You have it or you don't, and Jenny Fitzmaurice had it, and she was ours.

Behind the water tower, as our neighbors stared at our family and Mrs. Boerne ushered many of them away, Mrs. Fitzmaurice put her soft, elegant hand to the side of my head, she asked, "Are you OK, sweetie?"

And to this beautiful woman, with her dashing husband and daughter whom I loved, I said, "You don't know me, lady."

Victor was resuscitated at the hospital. Although he stayed at the hospital for four more days, he was able to speak almost immediately. Our father gave Victor a gentle hug and while he was down there I heard Victor tell him, "I stabbed that son of a bitch in the leg with his own knife." To which my father replied bafflingly, "I know."

Later I would ask my father what he meant by that—that he knew. We were all still under the impression that the man Abraham was still at large. It was not something that anyone could have easily misunderstood. The fact that he was still out there, with a knife on his hip, spread horror across the hill. It was a crisis. My father, however, denied ever even saying those two mysterious words to Victor.

Months later, on a weekend morning in early December, the two of us were sitting in the kitchen. The day was sunny but there was a foot of snow on the ground, so the light coming through the windows was white and blinding. When I pleaded with my father to tell me what he had meant, he said, "It's not an issue. That man is far away and behind bars now." Which was true as far as I knew. We had heard that Abraham had been apprehended and locked up in Stillwater.

My father was already in his suit, looking crisp and smelling of his sharp cologne—anise and cedar wood. His tie was in that immaculate knot I would try for years later in my adult life to replicate but never master.

"I just want to know," I said.

"You know everything I know," my father said.

"That's not true. There's something you're not telling me."

"You need to stop trying to see the ugliness in the world," he told me. "Focus on the good stuff. Focus on all these wonderful things around you."

The Cemetery Gardener

Approaching Lorna's grave, Doremeister removed his fedora, causing him to feel slightly naked against the breeze and tepid light, the sun low in the sky although it was hardly past noon. Behind him he heard the whisper of gardening shears at work and cautiously turned to watch, as people of a certain generation are wont to do at the sound of a project in development.

The gardener was trimming up the boxwood hedge by the drive—the last time he would need to do it for the year. It was a job the man would have done in a fraction of the time, Doremeister considered, if he were to use power shears. But there were still a few men around who could see that haste wasn't necessarily the best route toward a job well done. He was meticulous in his care, finding every stray sprig and leaf and removing it with a sharp snap of the blades.

Lorna appreciated the boys who worked on their yard on Cedar Hill. That home, still Doremeister's home, was precious to them from the start. Almost obsessively she cared for it—renovating, decorating, and repairing. It seemed her mission to make it the best home it could be, foreseeing changes well before they might be needed. As their son Ronald moved away to Swarthmore for college, she joked—although Doremeister knew that she was genuinely tempted to do so—that she was going to turn his room back into a nursery in the hope that it would encourage him to hurry up and marry so she could have grandchildren. Doremeister often felt it was the realization that she would never have grandchildren that rushed her to the grave, but that was only a fraction of the truth.

Prior to her falling ill though, they had some grand days in that home. Yes, there were rough spots when the reactionaries on Cedar Hill—with their cocktail parties till dawn—decided that nuclear power was evil. But he and Lorna persevered. No one could stay angry with Lorna. Her demeanor, so innocent and charming, quelled the most strident of cynics.

Using the headstone to brace himself, he knelt on the grass then pulled the brass vase from the ground and righted it, placing orange daisies inside. He situated himself to face her marker, examining the salmon-color of the granite, which she had picked out from a glossy catalog as she lay in her hospital bed. The headstone was sturdy, yet elegant and feminine, just like the woman herself. No, that wasn't true, Doremeister corrected himself. She wasn't as strong as he had thought, and that was the problem.

A patch of clouds was peeking over the eastern horizon, and a gust blew in seemingly from nowhere, as there were few trees where he was to warn of its approach. Doremeister wore his trench coat, but had yet to put in the winter lining. As he winced at the wind's bite, he saw in his peripheral vision that the gardener had cut the distance between them in half, now pulling crab grass at the base of an obelisk. Although it was difficult to tell for sure without looking at him directly, it seemed as though the gardener was watching Doremeister. Many years ago, a doctor in Nuclear Horizons' employ, whom Doremeister was told to see, taught him to examine why he had these kinds of feelings. What precisely was it that made him feel like the gardener was looking at him? Was it something in the whites of his eyes? In the tilt of his head? No, Doremeister decided, and therefore concluded it was all in his imagination.

He began praying to Lorna, but his mind wandered. Struggling to think of something new to report on their son, he recalled the winter Ronald tried to take up cross-country skiing. He must have been around twelve at the time, as Reagan was well into office, but they had yet to put Gorbachev in on their side. At one point in the first week he had the skis, Ronald stayed out a full day, returning home with a black eye, which he explained away as a result of falling down. Doremeister suspected, however, that it was from a run-in with the Jagger boys from up the hill. A snowball or a good old-fashioned punch.

A corporal shadow covered Doremeister, and he heard breathing. He turned to find the gardener staring down at him blankly, his mouth and eyes open at the same lazy aperture. He was stooped and mostly bald, the thin hair he did have pulled back over his spotty scalp, bringing to mind the carcass of a river animal. He wore a dark green shirt and trousers, just about the same hue as newly issued fatigues. He said nothing for several seconds, his shears hanging at his side. Doremeister's first inclination was that there was trouble here; that something wicked was imminent, but he was now better able to identify irrational conclusions. Doremeister boiled down the particulars of the situation—as he had been counseled—to find the more innocuous scenario.

"Am I in the way?" Doremeister offered, gesturing with his hands, thinking perhaps the man didn't speak English. When the gardener did not respond, Doremeister wondered if perhaps he didn't speak at all. A moron of some kind.

The man's mouth opened a bit more, and Doremeister shifted expectantly, placing his hand on the headstone. When still the man said nothing, Doremeister decided it would be easiest to simply move on.

"Not a problem," he said. "I'll just be on my way." Placing his hat back on his head and still bracing himself with one hand on the tombstone, Doremeister put his right hand up to the gardener for a bit of assistance, the kind of gesture that he found people of advanced years—regardless of mental capacity—accepted with a sort of instinct he imagined uniquely human. But this man did not make the slightest motion toward taking Doremeister's hand—a passive yet frightful act. Doremeister paused in that way, and felt his extended hand go cold. What do I do at this point, he wondered, here in this vulnerable position? Shall I try to ignore him, keeping my back to him and his shears while I struggle to my feet against the headstone?

"Are you the husband?" asked the man, stopping

Doremeister's breath with the words. He had an accent of some kind. Doremeister couldn't pinpoint it.

"I'm sorry?" said Doremeister, though he knew very well what the man had asked. It was a habit he had when he couldn't answer the question or was panicked.

The gardener lifted his shears to point at Lorna's headstone, and Doremeister flinched.

"Yes, the husband," Doremeister said.

"Doremeister."

"Yes." They stared at one another. A swath of dark clouds pushed in, squeezing daylight in the west. Doremeister caught his hat before it could blow off. "Listen," he said, seeing that it would be necessary to be firm with this man, "what exactly is it that I can do for you?"

The gardener smiled by lifting his upper lip as if he smelled something foul, a simian expression that made Doremeister want to call for help.

"What is it?" Doremeister demanded.

The gardener lifted his shears again, the blades slightly agape, and put one of the points to Doremeister's shoulder. Doremeister tried to move away, but he was at such an odd twist that it was impossible without impaling himself on the blades. His breathing grew heavy now; loud in his own ears with a slight whine deep in his ancient lungs. Still the gardener said nothing. Doremeister inhaled, searching for a passerby, which he did not find, yet still shouted, "Help! Someone please—"

The gardener jabbed the blade into Doremeister's

shoulder, the shock silencing him rather than causing him to cry out. Doremeister stared in disbelief at the blood. The gardener swung his shears casually at his side, and Doremeister's eyes darted over the field of tombstones, thousands of bodies and not a soul to save him. The gardener reached down and put his hand under Doremeister's injured arm. Although his pull was weak, it was enough to help Doremeister to his feet.

"Your car," said the gardener.

"I'm sorry?"

"Go to your car."

The gardener was smaller than him by several inches. His skin was umber; his eyes paler and lit from within. The man's slack expression was something Doremeister had always associated with the simple-minded, but he believed this was not the case here.

"What is it?" Doremeister asked yet again. "What's happening here?" Although Doremeister was seemingly starving for this information, he was quite certain he already knew the answer.

In the spring of 1986, Lorna decided to renovate their concrete cellar. Doremeister watched as she painted a series of color samples on the cracked walls. He was resistant to this new project of hers for some reason. The basement had the same pungent dampness as Doremeister's army footlocker, a moldy, not unpleasant scent that had a comforting effect for him, evocative of an innocence in his past that didn't exist. He would sometimes find himself wandering into the cellar for no reason other than to become immersed in that still air. But Lorna wanted something else out of that space.

"Do we really need this, dear?" he asked.

"Yes."

"But why?"

"For entertaining," she said.

"That's what the living room is for, isn't it?"

"Not everyone enjoys Hummels."

"What exactly do you have in mind here?"

"A place to socialize for goodness sake. Is it so hard to understand?"

"No, but with whom? What I mean is who will we invite to dance in our new ball room?"

She threw her brush to the bare floor, creating a deep red splash on the concrete. Seven tiny paint cans were lined up along the wall: one can a slightly brighter hue of red, the rest indistinguishable shades of off-white. She had new brushes as well, one for each color, neatly placed across the opening of each can. "Correct me if I'm wrong, but as I understand it, we're going to need space to entertain."

"I'm not following."

"From what I hear, they're beginning to take you in at corporate."

"Lorna. Sweetheart. I'm an engineer. They have no interest in engineers in corporate. At least not in the way you have in mind."

She picked up another brush and painted a wide

arc of ivory, much larger than her other strokes, using the full length of her arm, causing Doremeister to take a step back. "That's not what I hear," she insisted.

"Is that right? And where do you get this inside information?"

"*I* have friends," implying of course that Doremeister did not.

"I see. And which one acts as your Nuclear Horizons attaché?"

She said nothing, brushing a sandy-colored bit of hair from her face and wrinkling her nose in such a way that made Doremeister want to take her pretty face in his hands.

"Lorna," he said.

"Mrs. Boerne," was her answer.

"Ah, yes. I see. Well, that explains it, doesn't it? As Mrs. Boerne has no connection to Nuclear Horizons whatsoever and nothing better to do with her time but to invent—"

"Please do not insult that dear woman!" demanded Lorna. "She didn't invent anything. She heard it on good authority."

"Please, go on."

She turned to him quickly with the brush raised like a schoolteacher's ruler and inadvertently splattered a bit of paint onto his cheek. "You think I've got no idea what's going on over there? Do you think I'm so simple that I don't see it?"

"Good Lord. What are you talking about?"

"I know what a company like that must endure

to stay afloat. I know the kinds of people who court that kind of power. You think I'm a fool, but I'm not."

He took her gently by the shoulders saying, "A fool?"

She put her hands to her side.

"You know I don't think that," he continued.

She looked to her wall.

"OK?" asked Doremeister.

"Yes," she said and turned out of his hands to continue painting.

Regardless of where she got her information, Mrs. Boerne was right. Doremeister was working on something that was making him very popular at Nuclear Horizons and beginning to bring in a great deal of money for the company.

He had been visited by a man named Carl Johnson from the UK office. He wanted Doremeister to do a case study for a contract he had with Egypt via a Swiss organization called Institute for Advanced Technologies. He was to outline in detail the capabilities and use of something called Fuel-Air Explosives. Several things about this bothered him. Johnson looked and behaved as if he belonged on a used car lot somewhere, he rarely let Doremeister finish a sentence, and he wore pastel ties. But more to the point, the idea of allowing a foreign government to see defense-related material made Doremeister uncomfortable, and the FAE research itself was particularly suspicious. It was an old technology made with cheap components, but it had a big effect.

As a matter of course, Doremeister called the Swiss Embassy to find out about Johnson's IFAT, but they had no record of such an organization. And when Doremeister mailed a copy of the proposal to some fellows he knew at the Pentagon, they pointed out that the Egyptian government was never mentioned despite what Johnson told Doremeister. In fact, there was no end-user stipulated at all—only IFAT as the buyer—a troubling oversight, as it implied Carl Johnson was either hiding or lying about his intentions.

Doremeister recommended to his supervisor that Nuclear Horizons pass on the study on the grounds that it was against Nuclear Horizons' policy of withholding sensitive data from international organizations. His supervisor agreed with Doremeister, but upper-administration did not. Doremeister was to continue working closely with Carl Johnson and complete the study as requested, divulging any information Johnson required.

After a few restless nights, Doremeister did as he was told, but it was slow going trying to work with Johnson who was now back in Bracknell. Having a difficult time explaining just what was needed, Johnson suggested Doremeister meet with a few IFAT scientists. "Best to hear it from the horse's mouth," said Johnson on the phone late one evening.

"Very well. Set up a meeting here in Minneapolis and I'll be happy to—"

"I'm afraid that won't work, Doremeister. You'll have to go to them."

"Look, it's their study. Why can't they just—"

"It will be a nice trip for you. A little vacation. What's the temperature where you are now anyway? Ever been to Argentina?"

They picked him up at the Córdoba airport in a plush van that included in the back a wet bar and reclining seats but no windows. Two other men, one Hispanic wearing fatigues and the other Middle-Eastern in a double-breasted suit, sat opposite Doremeister, who sat with his back to the front of the van.

"More comfortable than a blindfold, I suppose" said Doremeister. It got a small smile from the one in the suit and nothing from the one in fatigues.

When he got out, he was in a cathedral of florescent lighting and craggy, gypsum walls. He was greeted by Johnson who quickly introduced him to the party of scientists. All of them relished his name. Delighted with the sound of it. Saying it properly, the way his father had. All of them clasping his hand with both of theirs. All of them German. Very old Germans. Specializing in poisonous warfare chemicals.

"Restroom, please," said Doremeister anxiously.

There was no pretense from that point. Johnson did not hide the fact that the study was not for the Egyptians, or that the men he was providing information to were former Nazis. Nor did Nuclear Horizons corporate try to hide the fact that this information was ultimately being sold to the highest bidder, who at that time was a fellow in Iraq by the name of Saddam Hussein. The thought of it steadily consumed

Doremeister.

In the car, his arm throbbing in pain, Doremeister managed to turn the ignition. The gardener sat in the passenger seat with the shears between his legs.

"What now?" Doremeister wanted to know.

"You will go home."

Doremeister scanned the landscape, now spotting several people, but off in the distance, too far for any of them to do anything in time to save him if he were to use the car horn or shout for help.

"I'm retired, you know," said Doremeister. The gardener looked at him. "I've got nothing to do with Nuclear Horizons, the Iraqis or any of that mess anymore." Again the gardener gave Doremeister his horrible smile, more of a snarl than something associated with happiness.

As Doremeister drove up Hennepin Avenue, a major thoroughfare in the city taking them through Uptown, he found he could not take advantage of several opportunities for escape. The gardener was an old man and would not be able to act quickly, but two things prevented Doremeister from taking action: one, Doremeister was an even older man; and two, Doremeister had—despite his bad arm—put on his seatbelt, a habit forced on him by Lorna. He would not be able to get his seatbelt off swiftly. Sometimes, with no pressure at all and two good arms, it took him several seconds to get the thing off. So he drove, wondering as they turned onto the parkway what the gardener had in mind for him.

"You loved her?" asked the gardener, the sound of his voice startling Doremeister. He glanced at the madman beside him.

"The missus. You loved her."

"Yes. My wife." Doremeister was having difficulty concentrating on the road. "Yes, I loved her very much." Why was this man asking about Lorna, he wondered. As he reached the stop sign at the bottom of the hill, just kitty-corner from the Goody home, a sudden thought occurred to him—this wasn't about Nuclear Horizons or the goddamn Iraqis at all. What was it he had asked? "You are the husband?"

One did not eat at Harper's Uptown Eatery. One dined there, and, when one dined there, one became immersed in the unaffected conviviality of the place. Harper's was the restaurant all other restaurants wanted to be: fine wood fixtures, heavy brass sconces, crystal tumblers, leather upholstery; a long, exquisite bar with bottles glistening, and bartenders in brilliant whites. Harper's was like a proper hat. It welcomed the wearer and improved with wear. What's more, each patron of Harper's believed that it was his own personal discovery; that it was part of his identity; it was *his* hat and fit no one like it fit him.

In the spring of '88 Doremeister was there to meet a Vice Admiral named Westchester who had come all the way from New Mexico to talk to him about a special project they were working on down there. Doremeister had agreed to meet with him because one year after he completed his work for Carl Johnson, things were becoming intolerable at Nuclear Horizons. A radical by the name of Mitsche and a group of protesters were drawing an intense amount of media attention to the company, mostly over cluster bombs. Doremeister was in constant fear that the work he completed for the Iraqis would soon be the focus of their cause.

Westchester made a tempting offer. He made it clear that Doremeister would no longer have to worry about the media. "At Los Alamos," said the general, "you'll be safe. At Los Alamos you'll find a home. And a family."

After Doremeister said goodbye under Harper's green awning, he went back inside and had a seat at the great oak bar, the low sun shining through the door and windows revealing cherry threads in the grain of the otherwise chocolate wood.

Doremeister was not a drinking man, nor did he enjoy being by himself. In fact, he never felt quite right if he was not with his wife. Yet that day he felt the only thing for him was to sit at that bar.

"A scotch please," he said to the bartender.

"Yes, Dr. Doremeister. Did you have a preference of scotch?"

Doremeister was caught off guard that this man should know his name. Who did he work for? What was he after? But Doremeister worked through it. This was just the way of Harper's of course. Everyone's special.

"No. Thank you. Just any scotch. Neat please." The bartender obliged.

Doremeister sat staring at the liquor bottles and felt the spring air, so foreign, brushing past him, as if on the way to tend to something important. It was not until her red wine arrived that he realized a woman had taken a stool beside him. It was Audrey Peterburg from Cedar Hill. She looked ready for the opera or ballet and smelled of it too.

"Hello, Doremeister," she said without looking at him. She blotted her blood red lipstick on a cocktail napkin then took a drink of her wine.

"Hello, Audrey."

"I didn't think you drank."

"Just not as much as some."

"Are you passing judgment?" Audrey wanted to know.

"No," Doremeister lied.

"What's the occasion?"

"Just having a drink is all, Audrey. You needn't concern yourself."

"The warmongering business getting you down?"

Doremeister took his wallet from his back pocket, resigned to make his exit.

"I've paid for it already," said Audrey Peterburg.

He glanced at her, putting his wallet back, and reluctantly thanked her. "I'm sorry," he added. "I didn't notice. I'm a bit distracted."

"I can see that. Is it Lorna?"

"Lorna? God, no. She's my salvation."

"Well, maybe it should be Lorna you're worried about."

He turned to her. "Now, what is that supposed to mean? Has it come to that? Have my neighbors become so ugly that you're now going to insult my wife?"

"No, Doremeister." He watched as she removed a large gold earring with her arching nails shellacked in red polish. She then placed the earring on the bar and rubbed her earlobe, likely weary from being pulled down by such a mighty ornament. "She's in trouble. You should have been able to spot it. But you've been absent, haven't you? Busy building your fucking bombs."

"What is it, Audrey? What are you getting at?"

"Drugs, you crumb."

"Oh, for heaven's sake. The lengths to which you people will go." Doremeister finished off his drink, and as he set it down, the bartender made eye contact with him. Doremeister nodded and another shimmering drink was placed before him; the old glass whisked away.

After Audrey had taken her time with another meticulous drink from her glass, she continued: "They've cut her off at St. Edward's. Not that it's stopped her. She still gets them. From where I wouldn't know."

"You disgust me," said Doremeister then stood from his stool, rage filling him.

"Doremeister," she said, still not looking at him. He tied the trench coat sash around his waist to delay his departure. "You're the one who likes to hurt people, not me. I'm telling you this because you're too dense to see it yourself and I don't want Lorna to hurt herself."

This was enough for Doremeister and he began to walk away, but she called after him again, "Doremeister!" He only slowed and turned his head slightly. "I'll get this scotch as well then, shall I?"

When he returned home, there was a note on the kitchen counter from Lorna telling him that she was out at Lund's picking up some groceries. He searched the medicine cabinet, her drawers, and the closet, telling himself all the while that he was doing it for her. He just wanted to be sure she was all right. And of course there was nothing. No illicit drugs beneath her underwear. Good Lord, the idea of it. How dare they? This was certainly crossing the line, perhaps the impetus to make the move to New Mexico.

Doremeister sat down in the chair across from the bed. He was suddenly exhausted; breathing heavy, eyes open wide. What was he expecting to find, a cache of drugs? But it wasn't that simple, was it? Not that obvious. And that's the reason he'd been able to deny it so easily up until now. Up until he realized the damned neighbors even knew about it. He leaned forward, putting his face in his hands, and felt as if he might cry, an absurd prospect for Doremeister. Then Lorna walked in, looking frail and skittish, as she had always looked these days, Doremeister so easily ignoring it. He couldn't hold it back and broke into tears.

It had started with Valium then moved over to Xanax, which she fell in love with. The things she was hearing about his work, and all the talk throughout the neighborhood, it tormented Lorna. She needed a little something to help her cope. Then, when Ronald went away to college, it was unbearable. That's when the dosages surpassed what her doctor at St. Edward's recommended, and she was told that she should begin weaning herself off the drugs, which was an incongruous suggestion in Lorna's mind. More is what she needed, not less. In the waiting area, as she came out in tears, a kind woman put her arm around Lorna to comfort her. She eventually explained to Lorna that doctors were forever under-prescribing. "It's a horrible problem. They're all so afraid of getting sued. But there are other ways, of course, to get what you need."

"Are there?" Lorna asked.

Doremeister was out of his element here. He knew Lorna needed counseling and that wasn't a problem. But she had gotten herself mixed up with this man who was selling her the drugs. She owed him a good deal, not so much that Doremeister couldn't afford to pay it, but he couldn't bring himself to give the man his money. Lorna begged him, but he refused.

"It's not as if he'll just write it off," Lorna explained. "He'll come after it." This unsettled Doremeister. He didn't have the tools to deal with this sort of problem. But he knew who did.

Doremeister went to Tom Peterburg of all people—husband to Audrey—certainly not out of respect for the man, but because he was the only person Doremeister knew with experience in this kind of ugliness. Peterburg was an attorney widely known to have successfully defended some of the most sordid people in the city, yet Cedar Hill embraced him because he kept political signs for the right fellows stabbed into his front lawn. Doremeister rather disliked the man, but in a remote way. For instance, it disturbed Doremeister to see him with his youngest daughter, still in pigtails. A man of his age having children—he was at least a decade older than Audrey—was somehow affronting to Doremeister. And always in suits, this man, as if trying to emphasize a point that escaped Doremeister. Yet, on that spring day when he went to speak with him, Tom was genuine and encouraging. He instilled a confidence that Doremeister didn't think was possible when dealing with a matter in which the variables, in his mind, were simply too scattered. A problem in which science did not factor in was a problem that made Doremeister feel untethered. But Tom Peterburg, it seemed, was privy to the proper formula, and if supplied with the necessary data, the solution was imminent.

After looking into things, Peterburg found that he knew the man who was selling the drugs to Lorna. He was a wealthy man named Sparks, running an operation worth hundreds of thousands of dollars. Peterburg advised Doremeister to just pay it off; put it behind him. Sparks was not someone Doremeister wanted to tangle with. But Doremeister refused. "I will not do business with a criminal," he said, and that was that. Peterburg could have easily made a snide comment about his work at Nuclear Horizons, but he did not.

Doremeister began to grow somewhat fond of

Peterburg as he filled Doremeister in on what he knew. Sparks had a mansion on Mount Curve, two children, a silver Jaguar with custom plates that read SP RX, and close relationships with civic leaders. Doremeister could see that it affected Peterburg; made him frustrated, even angry that such a man was taking advantage of Lorna and many others like her. When Doremeister asked how a man could be so successful in such a trade, Peterburg explained, "He is brilliant in his malice."

Sparks recruited the homeless to visit doctors and coached them on how to get the proper prescriptions. He stole prescription pads and printed his own. He manipulated pharmacists in a variety of ways. In one instance, in which he knew that the pharmacy had already been tipped off about his forged pads, Sparks called on a pay phone from the pharmacy parking lot. He claimed to be with the Minneapolis Police Department, and warned the pharmacist that a man was about to walk in with a forged prescription. He then asked the pharmacist to fill the prescription as quickly as possible. It was the only way they could catch the man, he explained. "When he steps outside, we'll nab him." Then Sparks walked in with his forged prescriptions, collected a supply of drugs, walked out, got in his car, and drove away.

Of course there was also simple robbery, where he could collect a huge booty of drugs, but this was rare for Sparks. He liked the graft. He favored the manipulation of people to get what he wanted. Of course it wasn't Sparks himself doing most of this work.

He was just running the show. Orchestrating the small army throughout the city to do his bidding. And what was more, Peterburg speculated that there was more than just prescription drugs on the line, yet he was a master at distancing himself from his own operation.

"Diabolical," said Doremeister.

They sat on Peterburg's front steps, Peterburg smoking a cigarette, Doremeister fiddling with his hat, and Audrey Peterburg spying through the window.

"I suppose he is," said Peterburg.

"To be able to get away with so much."

"Yes."

"How are we going to cut ourselves free of him?" Doremeister asked and then wondered if his "we" had been meant to include Peterburg.

Peterburg stamped out his cigarette in a geranium and leaned over to put his hand on Doremeister's knee.

"I'll take care of this, Doremeister," he said.

Lorna convinced him she couldn't make the move to Los Alamos and neither of them ever heard from Sparks again. But now, as Doremeister pulled into his driveway, it occurred to him that this was the man, after all these years, finally coming to collect his money. Perhaps just getting out of prison and taking the first opportunity to settle the score with the man who put him there. That must have been how Peterburg took care of the problem. Made a phone call and had Sparks hauled in.

Good Lord, thought Doremeister, how long has it been? Twenty years? The rage and frustration that must accumulate in a man after so long. After he robs my home, it will surely be curtains for me.

"What is your name?" asked Doremeister.

"Be quiet," he said.

"What would you like me to do now?"

"You will be quiet."

The man stared at Doremeister, the shears now resting in the space between them.

"Get out of the car," he finally said. "Go into the house."

Doremeister obeyed, having trouble with the keys at the back door, twice dropping them while the gardener breathed behind him. When Doremeister bent over the second time, the gardener poked him gently in the rear end. When Doremeister glanced at him, the gardener was smiling.

In the kitchen, Doremeister stood stock-still, his key raised and pinched between thumb and forefinger, while the gardener looked about the room.

"Sparks, is it?"

The gardener prodded Doremeister into the dining room, then the living room.

"Are you Sparks?"

He moved to the mantel and tapped one of the Hummels with the shears. "Who is it you think I am?"

"You are Sparks."

"Who is he to you?"

Doremeister dropped his keys into the pocket of

his trench coat and grasped his arm. The bleeding seemed to have stopped, but it still throbbed. He explained to the gardener who Sparks was, and how he had found a friend to take care of him.

Again, the gardener smiled. Now he took a framed picture of Doremeister and his son from the mantel. Staring into the photo, he said, "He paid it."

"Pardon?"

"Your friend paid the debt and you are a fool." The accent was Latin, South American, Doremeister thought.

"So, you are Sparks."

"I don't know this man." He put the photo back on the mantel, but still stared at it. "Your son is a gay."

Doremeister became nauseous with those words, and filled with hatred, more toward Ronald than the gardener. How had he known? Just from the sight of him? Was it so obvious? Doremeister sat gently in the armchair, still clutching his shoulder. No, he looked like any other young man. The gardener knew because that's why he was after Doremeister; Ronald and that mess he had gotten himself into. When was it? Just after they put Clinton in office, when everything went to hell. The sea changed from moral integrity.

Ronald struggled at Swarthmore. He could not seem to get his bearings and eventually came home for spring break and never went back. Doremeister argued and pleaded with him, but Ronald was adamant that he could not return.

"Then where?" Doremeister asked. "Which university would you prefer?" It enraged Doremeister that this was such a glib decision for his son. The lengths they had gone to get him into Swarthmore, and now he so blithely excuses himself. Ronald was not a stellar high school student. There was a spot of a year or two when he went through an odd identity crisis, dressing up like a vampire in long black robes and frightening stage makeup, but he seemed to straighten himself out by his senior year, and took classes to prepare himself for the SAT. Doremeister was able to pull a few strings and they were all thrilled when the letter of acceptance came in. But now it all seemed for naught.

"It's not for me," Ronald said, as if this explained it all.

"Right. Fine. Then which university is?"

"No, college I mean. College in general," said Ronald, and Doremeister stared at him dumbfounded.

For over a year, Doremeister watched Ronald skulk about, coming in at all hours of the night reeking of booze and marijuana, camped out in front of the television in the evenings when he came home from work. Ronald seemed to degenerate before his very eyes, becoming soft and overweight. The spark that was once in his eyes faded. Lorna only seemed to make it worse, catering to his every need and whim, taking meal requests and returning his laundry folded and ironed.

"You're not helping things," he told her. "He'll never leave if you keep this up." But she only smiled and shrugged. It did occur to Doremeister that their son's return to the nest might have actually been a good thing for Lorna, but he simply couldn't have it. He was very close to throwing him out on the street when Ronald came home during dinner one day and announced that he had a plan. He was going to start his own printing business. With his friend. Who already had some good equipment. They'd just need a little start-up money.

Doremeister would soon find that his son's perception of a little money was greatly disproportionate to his own. But Doremeister was willing to take the gamble. He was so thrilled to see Ronald finally motivated to do something that Doremeister hardly even considered whether or not the whole business scheme was such a great idea.

To save money, Ronald and his business partner, Terrance, lived in the warehouse in which they were running the business. Doremeister thought it sounded exciting. It made Lorna cry every time they spoke of it.

"It's what people do, Lorna," he would tell her. "When they're starting out. They struggle. It's a good thing for him. Can't you see how excited he is? He's happy."

And Lorna would have to reluctantly admit that, yes, Ronald did seem quite happy. They hardly saw him anymore, and when they spoke on the phone, Ronald would report brisk business. In no time at all, he was wearing new clothes and had a new car. It astounded Doremeister. He had always understood that the first year of starting a small business was brutal; it took a while to finally start making any money. Yet, Ronald and Terrance were clearly doing something right.

"You own this house?" asked the gardener.

"I own it? Yes, yes, of course I own it."

"No more mortgage?"

"No, it's mine. Look, I'm sorry if my son hurt you in some way. He made some mistakes when he was younger. He's made up for his past."

"You are such a fool. How are you able to afford such a house?"

"I'm not a fool. To you—with the weapon—I may seem foolish, but I can assure you I'm no fool. Please just tell me what you want. I can't understand how I could possibly make up for any wrong my son has done to you."

They were due to meet at the Torch-light Parade, just behind the tennis center, where they sat when Ronald was just a little boy. Lorna had packed a picnic of cold chicken and blueberry pie. They had a blanket spread out with enough room for Ronald and his friend Terrance. But they never showed. It ruined everything. The bass drums pounding in his throat, the pretty girls on the floats, the fat Shriners on their motorcycles, all of the things he loved about the parade were lost to consoling Lorna.

"He's a busy man now. This is a very good thing. He's got a business to run."

"Let's just go," said Lorna, already packing up the paper cups and orange pop. "Coming to a parade without one's children is silly."

Doremeister tried calling when they got back to have Ronald speak to his mother, but there was no answer. Nor were they able to get a hold of him the rest of the week. Then, at work, Doremeister received a phone call from a man identifying himself as a federal agent. He needed to speak to Doremeister about Ronald. He showed up at Doremeister's office five minutes later, making Doremeister wonder from where he had called.

"When was the last time you saw your son, Dr. Doremeister?" asked the agent. He was dressed in a dark blue suit that looked heavy, not only for the summer, but as if it actually weighed a great deal—stiff and thick. His collar was tight around his slightly fat neck, and he breathed heavily, like it was choking him. His skin where he had shaved was spotted with irritation, and he seemed scrubbed clean and pink.

"Perhaps you could tell me what this is about first."

"We believe your son may be involved with the production and dispersal of counterfeit money." Doremeister knew immediately that it was true. He considered that other fathers would be shocked and defensive at such an allegation about their son, but he knew, and it made him want to throw in the towel; give it all up somehow and walk away, like a failed project that just wasn't worth it.

"I'm not sure when I last saw him. Maybe a

month ago. He came home with a sack of dirty laundry."

The agent took some notes with his mouth open. When he finished writing, he gasped with a slight snort like he had just woken up. "So you were aware of your son's activities?"

"I was not."

"You didn't seem surprised when I explained why I was here."

"Perhaps I'll start blubbering when you leave the room."

Doremeister broke the news to Lorna when he got home, but she didn't believe any of it. She laughed at the prospect. That the FBI would think her son could be involved with something so sinister. Even when Ronald turned himself in three days later, confessing to the whole thing, she believed he was only doing so to protect Terrance. No matter what Ronald said to her to make her understand his guilt, she would not believe it.

When they bailed him out, and Ronald struggled to make her believe him, she said with a sly smile, "OK, I understand. I understand," then took his face proudly in her hands and kissed his cheek.

It was only at the trial that Lorna finally broke down. It was not the parade of shop-owners and victims who gave testimonials about how Ronald's actions ruined their lives or nearly brought their businesses to ruin. It was Ronald's admission, under questioning by an overzealous prosecutor, that Terrance was more than his business partner. That his homosexuality had nothing to do with the case didn't seem to matter. It was simply to illustrate to the jury just how degenerate Ronald and Terrance were. Lorna would never recover.

The gardener roamed the living room, examining things, admiring the room. "You have someone come clean for you," he said. "You are too good to clean your own home. Too important."

"I feel horrible about what my son did. But I am not responsible. I am not at fault. And he has paid his dues since that time. He was very young and very stupid. He's done everything he could to make up for his crimes. If you feel you deserve money you lost, this is not the way to get it. You will not find justice this way."

"Justice," repeated the gardener absently as he wandered back to the mantel. He picked up the framed photograph of Ronald. "This pink triangle on the boy's T-shirt. This is how I know he is homosexual." He tossed it to the ground at Doremeister's feet, cracking the glass into a Y. "You are a sad man, Doremeister."

Lorna, as it would turn out, found another doctor who was not quite as concerned about over-prescribing as her former physician. This one loaded her up with as much Xanax as she demanded. By the time Doremeister figured it out, again comfortable in his denial until it was obvious to everyone else, she was taking over one hundred pills per week. While Lorna clutched his arm pleadingly, he called the quack who was giving her the prescriptions and read him the riot act. He told him his wife was an addict and if he ever found out she was even in contact with him again, he would be sure to lose his license to practice. Then, still with Lorna at his side, her poisoned eyes glaring at him, he took a full bottle of the stuff and dumped them in the toilet. Each one was a darling size, made up of the same precious blue Doremeister would later dream of vomiting a steady stream of, never able to get it all out. She dropped to her knees and bawled as he flushed them away. They did not speak after that and the next day he went to work as usual, only to come home late in the evening to find his dear wife unconscious on the bathroom floor.

She had seized from withdrawal, they told him at St. Ed's, and now she was in a coma. She stayed that way for three more days and when she awoke there was serious damage. She could barely speak and feeding time was a chore. She could smile, but it destroyed Doremeister to see it. It was the smile of the dying—weak and relenting. They made final arrangements during the next four days, becoming the most honest and straightforward, Doremeister realized, that they had ever been with each other. But what was not said, although he knew it all too well, was that it was Doremeister who was to blame for her dying, for it was he who forced her withdrawal with his selfish rage, rather than wean her off the drug as it should have been. She tried to tell him, as he went on his rampage to purge the house of all that was indecent—the pictures of Ronald, Lorna's drugs, his awards from Nuclear Horizons—but he wouldn't listen.

Doremeister's mouth opened, staring at the photograph at his feet. It was taken a few days after Lorna's funeral, on his way back to California. Was this Ronald's idea of humor, posing with his father in gay attire to make them look like a couple? This with his mother still fresh in the ground. Did he talk about the picture on his father's mantel while at the gay bar with his friends, laughing at Doremeister's naiveté?

Doremeister kicked the picture with the toe of his shoe, sending it under the coffee table and beneath the sofa. The gardener laughed. It was a high-pitched laugh, but not loud; filled with raspy air. Doremeister did not look at him.

"Relax, Doremeister," said the gardener.

As if the gardener's words were more than rhetorical, Doremeister leaned back in the armchair, feeling a bit dizzy. The gardener ran his fingers along the mantel touching each figurine. He then went to the end table and placed the palm of his hand on the dome of a small Tiffany lamp Lorna had discovered at an antique store in Stillwater.

"How many times have I watched you visit your wife's grave?"

"Are you asking me?"

"A grave I have tended since before there was a body in the ground. Tended to more times than you have visited."

"Will you please just tell me what it is you want from me? Tell me how I can make up for any wrong you feel I have done to you."

"Make up, Doremeister? You want to make up for your wrongs?"

"So I can be done with you. So I can find medical attention." Doremeister grasped his arm.

The gardener stopped pacing and turned to Doremeister saying, "You do not recognize me. My name is Abraham."

"I'm sorry?"

"Abraham. This is amazing thing. Your life. So filled with guilt. So—what is the word? A mess. Buried under a mess."

"Cluttered," Doremeister assisted.

"That you do not even recognize me. I wanted you to see what became of me. After you did what you did. Or didn't do what you could have done. I wanted you to feel the shame you deserve. You didn't care whether or not I hurt that boy. You wanted only a chance to hurt someone. Anyone."

Doremeister was silent as he considered whether there was some sort of logic to what the gardener was saying or whether it was just the ramblings of a mad man. He still, despite the man providing his name, was not quite sure he understood. There seemed to be some sense to it, but his mind could not grasp it, as if it was just a phantasm. Many years ago a boy had been kidnapped from the hill, and Doremeister and another neighbor tracked him down and tried to ply information from him until the boy's father arrived and found out where his son was.

All of this for a faded recollection. But then, that apparently was the point this Abraham was trying to make.

The gardener moved on, pacing the room and swinging the shears at his side. "But you cannot feel any more shame. Your whole life is shame."

Doremeister sat up and gingerly pulled off his coat. There was not as much blood as he thought there might be, but he was still in a great deal of pain. He let his coat fall to the ground and grasped his arm below the wound.

The gardener continued his sermon. "Now I see. I may have become servant—serving those even after they have died—but you . . . A man defeated by himself. You are a *failed* servant. You have destroyed yourself. God has given me justice and I did not know."

Doremeister stood up but the gardener did not turn from the mantel where he was once again examining the Hummels. He picked up a figurine of a mother and father pulling their child in a sled, all of them smiling and rosy-cheeked. As Doremeister wandered to the kitchen still gazing at his arm, the gardener placed the tiny statue in his pocket. The water from the kitchen sink went on and the gardener turned slowly to see that Doremeister was gone.

As he passed the sofa, the gardener picked up Doremeister's coat from the floor. On his way through the foyer, on his way out, he stopped at the hall closet and carefully hung the coat on a wooden hanger. From the kitchen he could still hear water running, the flow into the sink intermittently broken as Doremeister ran a cloth beneath the faucet.

Vikings and Visigoths

"Your boy must be getting ready to head off to college soon?" asked Carl Rosenquist. He was with Doremeister, another man from Cedar Hill. They were teamed up, as nearly everyone from the hill had been that day, in a mad hunt to find a man and a boy from the hill he had snatched.

"Yes," said Doremeister. He was a sort of renowned grump on the hill and Carl resented having to spend time with him.

"Doing all right, is he?"

Doremeister shrugged. "I suppose so. Now. He seems to be making strides."

Carl nodded. Doremeister seemed to be always on the defensive, like a schoolboy who knew all the other kids were making fun of him behind his back. It was the late '70s, but Doremeister was a bit of a throwback by at least a decade, with his fedora and horn-rimmed glasses.

He was Carl's next door neighbor. They had a somewhat checkered past together, stemming from a dog named Randall, a golden retriever pup named after a boy Carl's daughter Molly had fallen in love with in her first-grade class. Randall the pup had abandonment issues, which manifested itself in howling and barking fits when he was left alone in the backyard.

"I understand that dogs bark," Doremeister wrote

in a note Carl found in his mailbox one morning, "I have no issue with that. My issue is with the fact that you perpetuate these rants of his by not reprimanding his behavior." He made a good point, or so it would seem. But according to Randall's veterinarian, it was only a matter of time before Randall became accustomed to being left alone, and if the Rosenquists were to go out and try to shush Randall every time he started to bark, they would in fact be enabling the problem.

As it would turn out, however, Randall would never get the opportunity to learn that lesson. Carl would find him dead one chilly fall morning, leaves blown into a pile at his little belly.

"And your little girls?" asked Doremeister, surprising Carl with the question.

"Oh, fine, fine. Molly's an athlete and Erin is our musician. Viola." Doremeister and Carl were driving down Hennepin Avenue on their way to another bar. They had been searching alleys on the hill, but decided that it was more likely the man they were looking for was holed up in a bar somewhere. It was a summer evening. Getting late now. They had the windows down, and a breeze blew in the smell of a Burger King as they passed it, though it must have been closed for hours now. Off to the east a police siren wailed for just a moment.

"Of course," Carl continued, "they're so young, I can't tell whether their interests are fleeting."

Doremeister, stiff behind the wheel, nodded. "Encourage everything," he said, and turned into Block E, filled with adult movie houses and strip clubs.

"Wow," said Carl. "It's almost like you know what you're doing."

Doremeister shrugged. "You want to find filth, you look in the garbage."

"OK then. Words of wisdom."

Doremeister glanced at Carl from the corner of his eye and pulled into the parking lot of a liquor store. They had all been given grainy Xeroxed copies of a photograph of the kidnapped boy, Victor Harper. Doremeister grabbed one off their stack, which was between them on the bench-seat of the Buick, and went to tape it to the outside window of the liquor store. The store was closed, but the parking lot was burning with floodlights, swarms of mosquitoes and flies littering the air. Carl stepped out and lit a cigarette.

"Any suggestions on where to look?" asked Doremeister as he returned.

Carl took a deep inhale from his cigarette and shrugged. "They're all the same to me." There were still a few people about on Block E, all of whom seemed like bad news even from a distance. As the night progressed it seemed to be getting warmer and there was a smell in the air of burnt motor oil and rubber. Carl slapped a mosquito on his neck, splashing a speck of blood across his skin.

"Blue truck," said Doremeister.

"What's that?"

Doremeister motioned with his head down the block and across the street to a small, blue pickup truck in the parking lot of a strip club. They had a vague description of the kidnapper—a dark-skinned man, short, dressed in all denim—and the vehicle he was driving, which matched what Doremeister and Carl were staring at, right down to the eroded, rust-covered wheel-wells.

They continued to stare at the truck, frozen in their pondering.

Carl threw down his cigarette and put it out under his foot. He glanced over his shoulder. Beside the entrance to the liquor store there was a payphone, scarred with filth and abuse.

"We'll call the police," he suggested.

"We can check it out first," said Doremeister and got back into his car.

Carl knew little about Doremeister other than that he worked for Nuclear Horizons as some sort of engineer and that he had been to war as a kid. Carl had always pegged Doremeister as a sort of passive fellow—the bookish type—but now, all gung-ho on this manhunt, Carl suddenly found himself in the position of envying Doremeister.

Carl's father went to war. As did his grandfather. They built their homes with their own hands. His grandfather worked the land his entire life to feed his family of 10 and died in his fields. His father was a foreman at Grainbelt Beer and a hunter renowned for his marksmanship and determination, once dragging a ten-point buck four miles across the snow-packed

Minnesota plains. They told exquisite tales of their adventures in the service, bar brawls, exploits and tragedies of youth. Carl used to look with awe upon the evidence of their hard-living: the color of fire in their cheeks, the cuts and bruises on their face, the scars that crisscrossed their bodies. Dye-cast hands; fists like mallets.

As a child, on a Christmas visit to his grandparents' home up in Winnipeg, his father and grandfather came barging in late one evening, barrel-chested and faces sweating although it was ten degrees below zero outside, laughing with blood on their faces and stony knuckles.

"What in God's name have you been up to?" his grandmother demanded to know.

"Tempering our Viking blood," answered Grandfather.

He—Carl Rosenquist, husband, father, now master to a schnauzer-poodle called Ike—worked at 3M, with a small office that overlooked the parking lot. The greatest achievement of his life—other than his daughters—was being part of the development of the "Sign Here" semi-adhesive tab.

Carl and Doremeister had the kidnapper in an open lot under an overpass west of downtown. It was hot now and dust and grit were blowing up in gusts from every direction. The light was dull and yellow, shining down from the sodium vapor lights high above on the interstate.

"You can tell us if he's alive," said Doremeister. "There's no reason why you can't tell us at least that much."

The man was breathing hard and sitting on the dirt with his arms wrapped around one leg. The other leg he kept straight because it was injured. He had a bloodied white towel wrapped tight around his thigh.

"Did the boy do that to you?" asked Doremeister.

"For Christ's sake, Doremeister, the guy doesn't even speak English. What do you want from him?"

"He does. They all do."

Carl laughed. "This is insane. We need to call the police."

"They won't be able to do anything. They'll have to follow procedures. We may not have the time to follow the procedures. We need to find that boy."

"Then Harper. We need to at least get a hold of Harper. It's his boy after all."

Doremeister turned and looked off toward the Mississippi, which was just over a hill to the east. He could smell it from there, in this heat. It was foul, like a boys' locker room and rotting fish. A semi roared and rattled by overhead. "Fine," he said.

"OK. I'll go to the payphone."

"No, I'll go," Doremeister said.

"What? No. Why?"

"It's my car."

"Are you fucking kidding me? I'll walk."

"You're also stronger than I am. He might be able

to overpower me." Doremeister was already walking to his car. He didn't need Carl's permission. "Wow," said Carl. "You are a piece of work, my friend."

Doremeister started his car then called out the window as he drove away, "Don't give him an inch."

Carl and Doremeister had abducted this man, Abraham, as he was being escorted out of the strip club by a grotesquely obese security guard. Abraham was drunk and even if anyone there spoke Spanish, he would have been difficult to understand. Spotting him immediately from the description, Doremeister pulled the car up to the entrance framed in neon lights. There seemed to be no name on the club anywhere.

"Get him," said Doremeister.

"What?" asked Carl, starting to panic.

"Get him! Get him!" Doremeister yelled.

"What the hell do you mean, 'get him'?"

"For crying out loud, Rosenquist, grab him. Get him into the goddamn car!"

Carl got out of the car, somewhat baffled and significantly terrified as to what was happening. He grabbed Abraham's arm and said to the bouncer, "I've got him. We've got him from here. He's with us," and ushered him into the Buick. Abraham was in such a drunken, confused state that it was easier for him to simply relent and hope for the best rather than fight at every turn. He yielded to his own abduction because right then nothing made sense, so what was happening to him was not particularly out of the ordinary at that moment, as everything seemed out of the ordinary. "Sorry," Carl continued, as he slammed the car door, and Abraham fell back in the seat. "So sorry for any trouble."

The bouncer—short sleeves rolled up over his fat shoulders, mouth hanging open—stared as Carl got in the car, and Doremeister checked for crossing traffic then carefully pulled away.

"Dondé esta el chico?" asked Carl under the bridge. Abraham stared back at him blankly, a bit of drool creeping from the corner of his mouth, his eyes nearly closed.

"Chingaté," Abraham mumbled.

"I know what that means." Carl stretched his neck. He stood before Abraham arms akimbo. "Sort of."

Abraham rolled over awkwardly, groaning, then began to push himself up.

"Oh, hey. Hey! Let's just stay put here."

But Abraham stumbled forward toward a pillar. Carl put his hand on Abraham's shoulder, which he threw off with a violent shake of his arm.

"You know what? Why don't you just relax, amigo?"

Abraham reached the pillar then leaned forward until his head made contact with a sharp pop.

"Ouch," said Carl.

Abraham undid his jeans and took a piss.

Doremeister first tried the payphone at the liquor store, but it was out of order, so he drove up the block to a phone booth, where he looked up the number for Josef Harper on Idyll Drive, then dropped a dime in and made the call. One of the daughters answered who explained that her father was out searching but would be checking in regularly. Doremeister told the young lady to have her father call the number he read off the telephone. Then Doremeister hung up the phone and stared at the black receiver as a bead of sweat broke from beneath the arm of his glasses and made its way down his temple.

In 1944 at the age of 17, Doremeister and his family were intensely patriotic. Although they were proud of America, their patriotism was also a defense against the prejudice against them for being German-Americans. Along with the pride they had for their country, there was also ire and fury for what was happening in Germany. His grandfather was the first one to come over, soon followed by his grandmother. They longed for their homeland, and Doremeister would often listen to them reminisce, but the ridicule he felt at school was unbearable. Even when walking through downtown St. Paul on the way home, grown men and women would shout at him, calling him a Kraut and telling him to go back to Germany. His blonde hair and blue eyes were a giveaway, as was the way he dressed: the meticulous needlepoint in his shirts, the finely pressed trousers, and the well-maintained sturdy leather of his suspenders and boots. His very bearing was German, though for his entire youth he never thought for a moment he appeared any different than his peers. Cleaner, perhaps. More well put together, but certainly nothing that deserved ridicule.

By the time Doremeister was old enough to enlist, his hatred for Germany was whole. He had an inner drive and focus to do everything in his power to help his country defeat them and put them in their place. He had a passion to find justice, a violence within him that he knew could be put to good use.

He was disappointed when he was assigned to the Army Corps of Engineers. And even more disappointed when the war ended shortly after he arrived and he was never even given an opportunity to fire his rifle in battle.

Carl was hugging Abraham as they stumbled through the dust—the hot wind whipping around them. A woman, hunched so severely that it seemed impossible that she could see where she was going, pushed a shopping cart down the street a few yards away. A tin can blew past her, clanging arrhythmically as it made its way down the street.

"Easy!" said Carl. "Just take it easy."

Abraham smelled awful, like livestock and sweat. The top of his head was black and wet. "No, no, no," he said, stumbling backward and then finally falling over, taking Carl with him.

"OK," said Carl. "That was fun. Maybe we could just rest here for a while. What do you think?"

And suddenly Abraham was snoring—sound asleep with Carl on top of him.

"Excellent," said Carl. He rolled off him and gently rolled Abraham over enough to reach in his back pocket and pull out his large billfold, which was attached to his belt by a chain. Inside there was a little over one hundred dollars and his passport. Carl looked it over.

"Guatemala? Holy smokes. That's a hell of a drive for a chica, hombre."

It was difficult to tell how much was true, and how much was just rumor, but the story was that this Abraham character had come up to take back his lover, who happened to be the thirteen year-old adopted daughter of Josef and Eloise Harper. Her name was Antonia. Carl knew nothing about her, but the story made him want to defend her somehow. He stared at Abraham's name in the passport for some time, then watched him sleep, wondering what the man's life must be like to have fallen in love with a child. He tried to imagine the world Abraham came from, but it was so foreign, he had no frame of reference.

Carl had had a minor breakdown in front of his wife the other day. Thankfully the girls were at a friend's house. He was down about work and she had tried to console him, but he wasn't having it.

"I don't understand why you're beating yourself up like this," she told him. "You should be so proud of yourself. You've done so much for 3M. And look at the lives you've made for us—for your family."

"I've done so much? You are referring, I assume, to the sign here tab. Yes, I must admit, the world is a better place thanks to my effort. Finally society can move forward. How we functioned prior to the sign here tab, I do not know, but now all those contracts and treaties and affidavits and bills and laws that have been piling up all these years can finally, *finally* be signed."

"This self-pity isn't healthy."

"No? Oh, well, God forbid I do something unhealthy. I mean, my life is so dangerous, I wouldn't want to add to the burden you must carry around with you worrying about me all the time."

"Is that what this is about? Your life isn't dangerous enough?" She gestured around the kitchen where they were sitting. They had recently had new orange Formica installed on the countertops and it reflected the sunlight from the window intensely. "This is all too damn boring for you?"

Carl put his face in his hands and mumbled, "Yes."

Doremeister knelt on the foreigner's chest and slapped him in the face.

"Dondé?" he yelled. "Dondé?"

The sun was just beginning to rise now making

the heat feel even more intense than it already was. Carl found a piece of rusted rebar and used it to whack Abraham's bad leg.

"Piece of shit," he whispered, as if more a reminder to himself than an exclamation toward Abraham.

Abraham wept from the pain. "Castillo," he cried. "El castillo."

A brown sedan came racing in under the bridge, raising even more dust as it skidded to a stop. Doremeister got quickly to his feet and Carl dropped the rebar with muffled clang against the dirt.

The car door flew open and Josef Harper came out in a huff. "What the hell is happening here?" he demanded to know. Josef was a tall man; thin, but formidable. It was something in his bearing—Lincolnesque perhaps. He was always crisp and pressed, yet seemingly prepared to split a chord of wood at a moment's notice.

"There's progress," said Doremeister.

"Progress?" Josef rushed over and knelt down beside Abraham.

"He's sobering up," Doremeister continued, "and beginning to talk, but he still hasn't told us where."

"Hasn't told you, or you haven't understood." Josef grabbed Abraham's shoulder and he winced. Josef looked up at Carl who shrugged.

"What happened to his leg?"

"It was like that when we picked him up," Carl answered.

Josef looked at the hand-tooled leather sheath on Abraham's belt and flipped it. "And his knife?"

Again Carl shrugged.

"Mi hijo," said Josef in a tortured accent. "Por favor, Señor. Dondé está mi hijo?"

Breathless, with tears muddying the dirt across his face, again Abraham said, "Castillo."

"Bastard," Doremeister grumbled.

Josef looked at him in rage.

"What?" asked Doremeister.

Josef sprang to his feet and ran to his car. "The water tower." Then added, not particularly quietly, "Idiots."

"Well, what should we do with him now?" asked Carl. But Josef slammed the door halfway through and sped away.

———————

Carl and Doremeister sped down 92 East with Abraham passed out in the back seat.

"You were pretty rough back there," Carl commented as he stared out the side window.

Doremeister looked at him, taking his eyes off the road for several seconds until Carl finally looked back. "You did your share," Doremeister said.

"Oh, sure. Yeah, I know. It's just that it really seemed to come natural to you. You didn't seem to have any particular qualms with the . . . brutality of it all."

"I don't recall having to beg you to join in."

Carl was silent on this for a moment. Abraham

began to moan in his sleep. "Had occasion to resort to this sort of physical tactic in the past have you?"

"I didn't kill your silly dog," Doremeister blurted out. "If that's what you're driving at."

"Who the hell said anything about my goddamn dog? I just thought with you being in the war and all . . ."

"I was on the engineer crew. I built bridges and roads. That sort of thing."

"Interesting, though, that you would bring up my dog."

"Oh, for Christ's sake."

Abraham started mumbling in Spanish and Carl turned to have a look at him. He was still asleep but he wore a pained expression and grasped at his leg.

"How much farther?" asked Carl.

"I just want to make it to the St. Croix."

"The St. Croix?"

Carl looked at Doremeister suspiciously, considering if Doremeister might have in mind dumping the man in the river. Doremeister would not give him the satisfaction of responding. If Carl wanted to think of him as a monster, so be it.

Carl and Doremeister had decided not to take Abraham to the authorities for concern that they might frown upon the tactics they had used to extract the whereabouts of the boy. They had also agreed that Harper was incredibly ungrateful, but that perhaps his rude behavior was due to the stress he had been under. Nonetheless, they were taking it upon themselves to take the foreigner to a remote location and to communicate to him in no uncertain terms that should he ever return to the hill, he would not find himself treated with the gracious hospitality with which he was welcomed on his first visit.

Suddenly Doremeister's head was grabbed from behind and Carl was struck in the nose with Abraham's elbow, though not hard enough to draw blood.

The Buick swerved off onto the shoulder then side-swiped the median. Carl, blinded with tears, grabbed Abraham and wrestled him into the backseat. Doremeister took the next exit, which led them to a park with a creek running through it. It was morning, the sun fully up, but apparently still too early for any activity wherever they were.

Doremeister pulled up quickly to the curb and jumped out. He opened the back door and grabbed the foreigner's feet. Together, he and Carl carried him to a set of jungle bars where they dropped him in the sand.

Abraham tried to run, but ran right into a bucking pelican on a large spring. Doremeister grabbed him and slammed his head against the yellow beak of the rocking bird.

"Hey," said Carl.

Doremeister ignored him, striking Abraham squarely in the nose, opening it up to a steady flow of blood beneath Abraham's trembling hands.

"OK," said Carl, but again Doremeister struck him, ramming Abraham's hands into his face. Abraham cried out, and Doremeister took him by the collar of his denim shirt and began pounding his head against the pelican, its smile coy and eyes looking up and back as if trying to ignore the embarrassing display going on down below—awkwardly ashamed of somehow being a part of this brutal punishment taking place. Rocking violently, like an autistic child in a panic.

Carl's home, as he walked in through the front door, smelled of fresh coffee and cinnamon-raisin toast. As he entered the kitchen, his wife, Annie, was pouring cereal for the girls. Molly was the first to see him and shouted out, "Daddy!"

Not to be outdone, Erin rushed to him and hugged him around his legs.

"Where have you been?" Annie wanted to know. "Why didn't you call? They found Victor."

"Good," said Carl taking a bite of the toast. "Thank God." He lifted Erin into the air by her arms and lowered her into her seat. Then he gave Molly a kiss on the top of her head.

"You smell," Molly said through a mouthful of Cheerios.

"I know, honey. Sorry."

"Why don't you go clean yourself up," Annie suggested, "and I'll have some breakfast waiting for you when you come down."

"That sounds good," he said.

But instead of coming down for that breakfast, Carl took a shower, lay down on their big soft bed, and fell soundly asleep.

As Doremeister dusted his toothbrush with powder, he recalled how the foreigner wept after Carl pulled him away. Despite the thrashing Doremeister had given him, they were not the tears brought on by physical pain. Rather, Doremeister thought, they were the tears of frustration—of complete despair.

Doremeister smelled the spearmint of the chalky powder then examined his tired eyes in the mirror, disliking the exposure his face seemed to have without his glasses.

What must it be like, he wondered as he slowly put the toothbrush in his mouth, to have that release—to enjoy that catharsis? To finally be able to break down and let go?

The Intrusion

As I sit there staring like a deviant through the windows at these strange people, I think they do not belong in my house. They do not understand that house. They do not deserve to believe that they somehow fit in the confines of that home. That home was ours on Cedar Hill. It was ours like our skin. For them to assume ownership is not so much an outrage as it is just an absurdity. They seem foolish.

It is evening. It is fall. A cool day getting colder with the falling sun. Tawny leaves rain down from oaks and maples. The smell is as I remember it: cold, damp earth beneath composting leaves; wood smoke; and academic promise. Warm light shines from the windows of the house and I can see them moving about playfully. Two children. No, three. The mother is at a computer. They are dark-skinned and thin. Eastern. When we were in that house there were seven children, although the two oldest were out of the house by the time I was ten.

The father is missing from this scene. As is a cat. There must be a cat somewhere in this life-size diorama, but it remains hidden from me, perhaps curled up on an ottoman or sitting in the darkness on a tree branch watching me watching this family.

Can those children appreciate this home as I do? Did I appreciate this home as I do now?

As I grow colder, hungrier, and wearier watching the scene of familial bliss before me, I want only one thing more. I need to get closer. I must feel the scuff marks we left in the hardwood floors, see the banister my sister Lucy got her head stuck in, and sit in the room where Antonia used to sleep. I foolishly think for a moment that her bed will still be there; the yellow dresser where she kept her clothes; and her orange, terrycloth robe hanging on the hook on the bathroom door. Even so, I must see those things no longer there. I suppose I could knock on the door and explain myself, and I would likely be welcomed inside and given a tour, the father a domestic docent lecturing me on tankless water heaters and granite counter tops; but I could hardly endure it. My need is for solitude with that home—quiet so I can hear it breathe, stillness as our past comes to the fore.

In the morning, I drive from a motel uptown and park my rental car beside the lake. Nothing much has changed here. The city has done some work to tame the frequent flooding of the path on the north shore, but their efforts seem to have been in vain. The grassy areas are saturated and several trees list precariously, their roots unable to find purchase.

The clothes of the people roaming around the lake have changed after all these years from baggy sweatpants to lurid Spandex. But the geese remain the same: loud, territorial, and shitting everywhere.

I make my way to our home on the hill. The sun

is out and it's rather warm for the season. I carry my jacket across my arm. I cut through the alley and am pleased to find that it is still paved with cobblestone. Those stones were a novelty when I was a boy, now they are downright historic. Little has changed, but the influence of television shows about home improvement and real estate is apparent. The yards are groomed in a more precise way than when I was a boy, and the homes themselves are freshly painted, with vinyl windows and gutters. Two assholes have sacrificed healthy portions of their yard for additional garage space.

From a distance, I hear commotion up ahead—chatting, but not the festive banter of a cocktail party. The mood and tone are curious and I cannot quite pinpoint what it could be until I see it and then it seems obvious. A garage sale is underway in what used to be the home of Ernest and Margaret Mitchem. The yard was tidy back then with tulips and forget-me-nots in spring, but now it is an extravagant affair of layered landscaping and sectioned gardens that seem to have distinct themes. A sundry of people wander about the yard opening bureau doors, inspecting kitchen appliances, thumbing through albums and CDs, browsing books, holding up shirts to each other's backs. The people are black, brown, and white; old and young; and rich and poor. The rich are from the neighborhood, Cedar Hill. The poor have read about the garage sale in the paper and have come to claim the luxuries of the rich at a fraction of the price. A pretty woman sits on the back steps watching the crowd with a look of disgust. She drinks a glass of white wine at this early hour and seems on the verge of shutting down the whole operation. A dashing man who could only be her mate, rushes about making the sales and answering questions. His teeth are stupendously shining from his smile.

I hear my name.

"Victor?"

And turn and see before me Janice Heikenin. How I can identify this woman after so many years, I do not know. I'm sure I have changed in ways I have not realized over the years, but she is a completely different person—thinner actually and well-saloned with expensive hair, but she is withered and on edge, worried about when it will all come to an end, or more to the point, what she will do when it does. Yet I see her in there, inextricably that girl I went to high school with.

"Victor Harper?"

"Janice Heikenin."

She embraces me with a force that catches me off guard. She is sincerely pleased to see me. As we move apart I see that she is teary-eyed. Why on earth has she had such an emotional reaction to seeing me here?

"My God, Victor. My God."

"Janice Heikenin," I say again stupidly.

"Goody," she says.

I am confused and she sees it in my expression, but she's deliberately set me up as she has likely done dozens of times in the past.

"Janice Goody. I took my husband's happy name." She waves her heavy ring set quickly through the air. "Those are mine," she continues, gesturing to two children. "Martin and Kirstin."

The boy sits under a tree playing some sort of hand-held electronic game. The girl sits on a stoop in the doorway to the garage texting on her cell phone with an indignant expression on her round face. They are both sullen children with dark hair and the dull eyes of television addicts. They are soft and pallid like blobs of dough, but not as friendly.

"Wonderful," I say.

"Peggy! Peggy! I want you to meet Victor Harper. He grew up here on Cedar Hill."

I shake hands with a small woman with a particular strength around the eyes.

"Back for a visit?" asks Peggy as she is clobbered in the hip by a little boy with Down syndrome. His twin follows behind sandwiching his brother against Peggy's faded Levis. Peggy arranges them one on each side of her and introduces them as her sons, Lars and Gustaf. Lars has a brace on his foot. Gustaf has a bandage over the top of his ear. They smile, look away bashfully, and then extricate themselves from Peggy to rush away.

"They're here selling their wares," says Peggy and turns aside to reveal a folding table arrayed with a bizarre collection of items. It looks a great deal like a museum installation of found items. A turtle shell, a beat-up Tonka truck, a tobacco pipe.

"From their adventures around the neighborhood," says Peggy.

I pick up a roller skate and spin the wheel.

"In the park?" I ask.

"The park, along the railroad track, behind the water tower. Anywhere and everywhere. But we're turning over a new leaf. Liquidating the inventory and no more unsupervised missions. Lars had a run-in with a steel-jawed trap."

I wince. "Lord. Where?"

"Railroad tracks."

I put down the roller skate and pick up a set of rusty mitten clasps.

"Victor grew up in the Krishnamurthy's house," Janice says.

"Krishnamurthy," I repeat.

"They are the sweetest family," Janice tells me. "You should be so happy such good people live in that home now."

I wonder absently about any nefarious items that have been left off this display. The drug paraphernalia, the condom, the porno magazine that Lars and Gustaf must have brought home and Peggy quickly did away with. And that's when I see the knife.

"This house is bound to go up for sale any day now," says Janice. "If you're in the market to move back home."

"So, tragic," says Peggy.

"Her husband committed suicide," Janice explains. "After she left him. For that dick." She gestures to the man with the wonderful teeth.

It is a hunting knife with a slightly garish curve in the spine of the blade and a faded insignia of a scorpion on the handle. It smells of wet leather and rust. Like so much else in my world right now, it has changed with the many years, but I know this blade intimately. As would the man I stabbed with it a lifetime ago. As Peggy and Janice ramble on about the eccentric man who once lived here, his cancer, and the pretty, sad woman with the white wine, I am in a trance recalling that day so many years ago when my actions turned this community upside down.

At the age of eleven I was a local celebrity for being taken from the hill. Abducted by a stranger in his truck and taken behind the brick water tower where I was beaten into a coma. Our neighbors turned out in droves to find me, and for many years afterward I was defined by that event. The kidnapped boy. Perfect strangers would feel they had a connection with me, though not perhaps as one might think. Their imagined bond was one of indignation. Some mutual sense of injustice. They wanted to share my anger and hatred for what happened to me. Relay how angry they were that such people existed in this world, so I would know that they saw the ugliness in this world that I had experienced. "It's awful," they would say, "that there are people like that in this world. Why they can't just do something about this I do not understand." And invariably at some point the words were spoken outright, "It just makes me so angry."

What they did not know, however, was that what

I felt was not anger. What I felt was shame. And it was not shame for anything that was done to me. I was no victim.

I arrive at night. Glancing into houses as I pass by brings a rush of nostalgia as I remember a time when I felt like the whole world was as sound and sturdy as the homes that dot this community. They are large, but tasteful and each unique from the other. It is a community built over time rather than by force of an outside party's drive for quick money. It has an established elegance that is rare in this country and occasionally razed for "bigger" and "more." Looking at the Midwestern, German-influenced architecture is a joy to me and lends me some small comfort knowing this pleasant part of my past still largely exists.

Our home is complex in its architecture with an asymmetrical design that creates a sort of visual mystery. Not able to take in the home as a whole, one wonders about what one doesn't immediately see.

Gray slate covers the cross-gabled peaking rooftops. Tall single-hung windows with nine-pane top sashes are scattered about and line a large sun porch jutting out to the west on the main floor. Just beside that porch, a broad brick chimney rises up past the third story where Lucy and Antonia's suite was.

The basement has several hard rooms, all encased in damp concrete. Cold and gray, yet filled with good memories, there was the laundry room, my father's work bench, my brother Graham's weight room, a room used as a general-purpose play space over the years, and two coal chutes. It is through the window to one of these chutes I mean to sneak into the house. I recall other windows I was able to crawl in and out of as a boy, but the coal chute is the least conspicuous and of course I am not as limber as I once was, so climbing the house, while tempting, would be unwise.

When we lived here we used one chute to store our storm windows or screens depending on the season, and the other one for firewood. Hoping that the Krishnamurthys have not yet purchased their wood for the winter, I choose the latter.

I pry the lock as if no time has passed, and shine a penlight inside to see that there is no firewood, but instead a tangle of beach toys and infomercial exercise equipment. I lower myself down and am able to slowly squeeze through, but I am making too much noise. I pause and hear movement on the other side of the door. Someone listening to me listen to them. We are both frozen, listening. Then the loud cry, "Mom!" And footsteps rushing up the stairs. What on earth is that child doing up so late? It's nearly eleven. And what could she be doing in the cellar?

I quickly debate how to proceed. How will the mother react? Will she believe the little girl? Will she think it another instance of an overactive imagination? Will she chalk it up to the creaky bones of the old house? I decide to wait it out.

Five minutes later, no one has come to investigate

and I move on, slowly turning the knob and pushing the door open. Light shines in through the crack and I peer through into the mise-en-scène of my youth.

But, oh, how things have changed. Plush, dense carpet runs through the hallway and golden sconces line the walls. Reds and browns abound like the den of a baron. Clean air smelling of synthetic products rushes down the corridor and there is soft music coming from the end of the hallway.

The horror.

I leave footprints in the carpet as I walk down the hall, away from the stairs, toward the music. Life moves above me. Creaking, thumping, mumbling.

At the end of the hall, the room that was once filled with the smell of sanded wood and my father's well-worn tools is now what I have heretofore only heard tell of: a scrapbook room. An entire room dedicated to the wretched yearning to arrest time with ribbons, glitter pens and a hot glue gun. No, the hypocrisy of my disgust does not escape me.

To the left, where Graham's weight bench was—where I would watch him in awe as he repeatedly pressed more weight than I was able to push off the bar—there is now yet more gimmicky exercise equipment including a treadmill and a step climber arranged before a large flat panel television attached to the wall. But this is not where the music is coming from. It comes from the room across the way where an even larger television is set up before a massive curving sofa. Playing on the television two teenagers dressed in exquisite, formal attire kiss in what appears to be a penthouse with a view of the George Washington Bridge.

Someone is coming.

"OK," he says firmly, and then, "No."

He's walking down the stairs. I cannot get to the coal chute in time. There are no closets to hide in down here.

"Because Favre won't have the endurance."

No bed to hide beneath; no wardrobe to duck into.

"Then you take him. I'm looking for a running back anyway."

My only option, pathetically, is to hide behind the door.

"Look, don't try to sell me on it. I know what I need, and I know what you need."

I see him briefly as he passes the crack. He is heavier than the rest of his family; average height. He smells of chicken and Aveda.

"I'm not doing this. I'm going to bed."

Foolishly I peak around the corner to see if he will sit down, but he grabs the remote from the lacquered coffee table and switches off the TV.

"Fuck you."

He pockets his cell phone, switches off the light and mumbles, "Asshole." As he makes his way back upstairs.

I am cast into the dim light provided by the glowing Sony display on the TV and the tiny lights in the collection of media equipment below it.

When Abraham, the man who ostensibly abducted me, came to our home, he had come for Antonia. Antonia and I spoke with him in the front foyer with my brother Walker eavesdropping over the upstairs railing. Our parents were out.

Abraham was brick red, the flesh around his eyes meaty and strained. Dressed in denim with that knife on his hip, he was determined and firm but not unkind as he told us in Spanish that he was there for Antonia. When she refused to go with him, he said he would be back when our parents returned.

You will have to understand here, the idea of losing her was horrifying to me. She had quickly become something I would not live without. This man, though I knew well who he was and his legitimate reasons for being there, was a monster to me. Antonia had told me that he may come one day, and we had read aloud his letters pleading with her to return home. Her mother had put Antonia up for adoption while her father was traveling in a search of work. Antonia insisted that her mother had had no choice because they were so destitute. Her father explained in his letters that there was enough money to care for her now, but Antonia feared that if she were to return, word would get out what her mother had done and they would be ostracized. The story back in her Guatemalan village was that Antonia had been sent to live with family in America, but if Antonia returned, surely her new American family would cry foul and the

213

village would soon learn the sordid truth.

Yet, even with this knowledge, I had no sympathy for her father, Abraham. I wanted him gone; wiped from the face of the earth to erase any possibility of losing Antonia.

The light on the alarm system console is red for armed. I heard the beeping from the basement as it was set. It seems there is no motion detection, likely to accommodate that cat I sensed before and smell now. Nonetheless, it doesn't look as if I'll be able to leave this house undetected.

I sit at the kitchen counter. Sure enough the countertops are granite and there is new cabinetry. The kitchen floor of my youth was linoleum with long gashes throughout from a winter our father flooded the back yard to make an ice rink and neighbor kids wandered in with ice skates still on. The floor today is some sort of stone, but it's difficult to make out in the dark. I guess travertine. The countertops had been green Formica. On the breakfast bar there was a small burn shaped like the state of Illinois that was caused by a marijuana one-hitter that Walker left burning as he fell asleep at the counter. No such ugly scars exist in this kitchen.

The kitchen is where we gathered for cards, homework, and conversation. It was the one room in the house with a window-unit air conditioner. I'm not sure if it was the air conditioner that brought us together or that we brought the air conditioner to where we gathered.

Our father was not home often. A well-respected restaurateur, he worked hard and late to maintain the best restaurant in the city. At night, he would come in through that back door from the garage, as neat and dapper as when he had left in the morning. Even now, it baffles me how he could keep himself so well put together in such a gritty, steamy business.

It does not smell of food in this kitchen. It smells of perfumed cleansers and plastics—closer to the shoe department at Macy's than a kitchen. Standing over the sink I look out to the backyard. Although I am unable to see the yard now, I know from my previous reconnaissance that it is similar to how we left it. I would like to open the window, breath in the night air that surely couldn't have changed so much over the years, but I see that there is an alarm sensor on it.

In the fridge there is an inexpensive, opened bottle of pinot grigio, and I am pleased to find that the drinking glasses are in the same cupboard. I pour myself a tall glass of wine and continue my tour.

As I enter the sun porch, there is just enough light to finally reveal that cat. It stares at me from a chaise lounge. In this room, maybe around the same time of night, I once came across my brother Shepherd, home from his first year in college, making out with Jenny Fitzmaurice, a girl he was in love with throughout his adolescence, yet never once had he be able to reach out to her until that fateful night. God, how I envied Shepherd that night. Jenny's long dangling arm in the air, the arch of her foot resting on his calf. Shepherd's hand laced in that wavy blond hair, cupping the back of her head. I swelled with pride.

When Abraham left our house, I jumped in the bed of his pickup. He pulled over at the brick water tower not far from our house. When he came around to the bed, I threw myself at him. Though I was not big, I took him down onto the chamomile and dandelions, dust filling my nostrils. I struck him several times before he got to his feet.

Abraham walked backward telling me in Spanish that he didn't want me to get hurt. That I needed to go home. He and my parents would take care of this. When he stumbled over a brick, I pounced on him again, and Abraham grabbed me by my shoulders and pinned me to the ground saying, "Solemente quiero mi hija." I only want my daughter.

It was at that point that I took his knife from its sheath and jabbed it deep into his muscled thigh until I hit bone.

In the upstairs hallway, a light shines from beneath the bedroom that was my parent's room. The adjoining room was my mother's study where she wrote her popular column for the Minneapolis *Star*, but there is no longer an entrance from the hallway, and I realize with a sudden queasiness why that is. That room has undoubtedly become a walk-in closet and master bath.

The room to the left, I wager, belongs to the youngest girl who may at this moment be cowering under her covers from the intruder she knows is in her home. The cedar-lined room to my right is likely the little boy's room, and upstairs, with her own bathroom, is the oldest daughter. It is there where Antonia slept.

Listen to me. You would have to see the skin on Antonia's arms. I cannot call it color. I cannot call it texture. Yet there is no softer affect, no gentler image than those tiny, downy hairs against that gold-brown field. You would have to see the crease at the corner of her left eye beside that pearly pool of infinity. You cannot understand without staring at the curl in her upper lip and the fineness of her ankles. If you hear the random creak in her voice when she speaks and the shocking gusto of her laughter, you may begin to understand. And to hear the effortless roll of her Spanish and the way she runs into a chilly lake, you will get an inkling of what she is; what I feel for her. But it is not that brand of love. It cannot be. She is my sister.

After Abraham pulled the knife from his thigh and tossed it aside, I went for it again. It was the last thing I remember until waking in the hospital. Through certain details and the injury to my hand, I pieced together that Abraham threw me aside into the wall of the water tower in a jerk reaction to protect himself from the murderous boy that I was.

After I was discovered, there was a manhunt for Abraham. Neighbors gathered and scoured the city looking for the man who tried to kidnap Antonia and beat the poor Harper boy to the brink of death. We were told days later that he had been apprehended outside of the city and was in jail. I have my concerns, however, that it did not end so neatly.

Antonia and I had concocted a story well before Abraham ever arrived. Two rotten children carelessly plotting the destruction of a man's life, we told everyone that he was not Antonia's father, but was instead there to take her back to Guatemala to be his bride, like an evil prince in a fairy tale. It left us giddy as we invented the tale and we did not fully realize the effect the story would have on those who heard it. The mere thought of such a despicable offense brushed everything else aside, including reasonable thought, so their emotions could swell with disgust and anger. Odium spread across the hill like a virus.

And a rift of sadness formed between Antonia and me.

———

Here is where she once slept. Where Krishnamurthy's long-limbed daughter sleeps now beneath a yellow-flowered comforter. The cat has followed me up here. It jumps on the foot of the bed, turns to me, and stares.

Is it possible that one can actually experience the

love that one recollects? Does that love exist? What I felt for Antonia I sometimes wonder if I will chase forever. Not Antonia, but what I felt. Was it even real or does it only exist in my reverie?

Krishnamurthy is on his way up the stairs. I can hear him walking slowly. I know it's him from the weight of his step, and I know he knows I am here from the cautious pace.

Not long before Abraham came to take his daughter back, a boy climbed our house to get to this garret room I stand in now. He was there to woo our sister, Lucy, who shared this room with Antonia. Boys were forever falling in love with Lucy. I consider attempting that climb now to escape, but decide it's too much of a risk.

Krishnamurthy enters the doorway, wild-eyed, wielding a bat over his shoulder. He is out of his mind with terror and will have no problem bashing in my skull. There is no explanation I could give, no reasoning or pleading will get me out of this situation.

From my back pocket, I remove the scorpion knife. This does not ease Krishnamurthy's temperament. He breathes heavily, spittle shooting from his mouth, but he still says nothing, and his daughter still sleeps. I edge toward the door and he steps toward his daughter, away from the door.

And here I am, with this damn knife, a misunderstood monster like Abraham. And yet perhaps, I am not so misunderstood.

Mercy

Antonia ran down Lake Street, her two-inch heels smacking against the sidewalk. She wore a black skirt with a simple pattern embroidered at that hem just at her knee; a pale trench coat tied at her waist. She had never been much of a runner. She had tried with her brothers, but never found the passion or solace or whatever it was that drove them. But now, she ran. She ran for the train. And although she rode the light rail frequently, she had never run to make a connection. She was never the sort to feel rushed. This train was an exception.

She had been at lunch with a friend. When she came back to her apartment, there was a package waiting for her with a note. She asked the doorman when it had arrived and he told her she had just missed the delivery. She did not see the writing on the envelope until she was in her apartment.

Antonia knew many men, several of whom had been her lovers and many more who wanted to be, yet when she saw the writing on that envelope—her name only—she knew it belonged to none of them.

She had not seen her father for over thirty years and she could not recall a specific incident when she might have seen his writing—he was a common laborer when she was a girl in Guatemala—yet she knew as soon as she saw it, that it was from him. The letters were crooked and pressed hard into the paper, showing deliberation and strain. Inside the envelope there was a note written in Spanish with the same self-conscious scrawl. It read, "Was thinking of you when I saw this. Your father, Abraham."

Antonia opened the small cardboard box and found, wrapped in newspaper, a Hummel figurine of a mother and father pulling a child on a sled. She stared at it, perplexed. So utterly unlike anything they had experienced as a family. A white ideal, captured in white porcelain.

Her apartment was sparse in a fashionable way—clean surfaces with bold angles in the architecture. The decorations were minimal, but where they existed they were of South American design, applying an agreeable juxtaposition to the modernity. The Hummel figurine had absolutely no place in such a setting, even as a piece of ironic kitsch. Was it intended as a slight against her, being raised by a white family? She set it dead center on her weathered coffee table and stared at it for a moment before it occurred to her that she could catch her father before he disappeared from her life again forever.

Many years ago she had forsaken Abraham to save her mother. And herself. She had denied him as her father so that she could have a chance at a comfortable life. She had hoped that he would simply move on, put the life when he had a wife and daughter behind him; let Antonia and her mother realize their plan for a better life, allowing herself to be adopted by a wealthy white family, but she knew in her heart that he would never be able to do that. She could feel his anguish. In the happiest and most hopeful moments of her life, the guilt would eventually consume her and she would think of Abraham and his empty life. She would see him clearly in her mind, defeated by life.

As she ran, her trench coat whipping in the fall wind, she wondered why she had been so certain that he was taking the train. He could have a car. He could have taken the bus or a cab. Why the train? Because it was the only hope she had of catching him. And so she ran, her feet aching and her breath strained; her hair black like wet ink flowing behind her. She could see the Metro Transit station, and as she looked for traffic, she hopped from the curb and her heel snapped off. She went down, skidding onto the asphalt. Her lovely knee and the palms of her hands took the brunt of the fall. As the lights turned and traffic approached, several people rushed to her aide. Low clouds moved swiftly overhead and the sun suddenly shined down brightly.

She insisted that she was fine despite the blood, and while on the ground, she slipped off her shoes before she got quickly to her feet and began running again.

When he hadn't showed for her mother's funeral, she took it as a good sign. She was pleased with the idea that he had finally given up on them. That he had moved on and had only scorn left in his heart for both of them. She was desperate to make him into a monster. Perhaps not as awful as the monster she had made him appear for her American family and others in their community—an abusive pedophile who she should be protected from at all costs—but a monster nonetheless who had no business being in her life. But it was a delusion, she truly knew. Had he truly grown hateful, he would have turned her mother in long ago, finding pleasure in her arrest and subsequent abandonment by all her family and friends who had simply thought Antonia had gone to stay with distant relatives. But he never did, and now he was almost certainly a poor man and it would have been an impossibility for him to make it home for the funeral. She knew from her mother than he had never returned to Guatemala, and Antonia could feel that he was near her.

She watched from a block away as the train pulled under the shelter, smooth and clean, slipping in almost without a sound. She was exhausted now and in pain, but went on, hoping there would be a delay.

He had known where she lived, re-enforcing her suspicion that he had been watching her. For how long? Had this been his concession to her disavowal, being a part of her life without her knowing it?

At the shelter, she approached the open doors of the train. The wind swirled here, grabbing trash from the overflowing bin. Her breathing was heavy. She felt like a mad woman, the soles of her feet now dirty against the patterned brickwork. But the looks she got from passers-by were of concern, not trepidation, for she was still beautiful despite the scraped knee and windblown hair.

On the train, she felt the grooves of the hard rubber on her feet as she walked down the aisle. The place was engulfed in an antiseptic hum, light, and odor. Her heart was racing and she felt as if she might collapse. Her actions had been so irrational. That he would be on this train was absurd. And yet, as she looked to the back, there he was. Sitting with his back straight, in a green workman's uniform. He did not seem to see her as she took the open seat across from him. Then as she stared at him, his skin so dark; his eyes so old, he looked to her. He seemed not surprised or taken aback in the least. His eyes that had seen so much sun looked at her from head to toe. He reached in his back pocket and pulled out a white rag. Even as tears fell from her cheeks, he seemed without emotion. And as he held the rag to her knee, he whispered, "Pobrecita." Poor little girl. Cupping her injured, beautiful knee with his aged hand like dried clay, "Pobrecita."

Author Bio

Emil Kresl was born and raised in Minneapolis, Minnesota, before going off to college in Madison, Wisconsin. In both places there was lots of laughter, stories, and swimming. In Madison he learned how to write fiction and plays, and picked up a thing or two about philosophy.

He paid his way through college tending bar and cleaning up apartments after rent-jumpers. After college he tried a stint working in politics, but opted to return to running a bar where colleagues are loyal, the excitement is frequent, and the stories slightly less absurd.

After Madison, it was off to Hollywood where he learned about screenplays and swimming in the Pacific Ocean. Then a couple years later, he went off to Austin, Texas, to see what all the fuss was about. There he found the best swimming water he had ever seen. He also got to work with some of the best storytellers around, found the love of his life, and helped bring into this world a human of astonishing beauty, wisdom, and good humor.

To put food on the table, Emil helps people find happiness and fulfillment by contributing in a meaningful way to the world around them, which is not a bad way to collect a paycheck.

When he's not doing all that other stuff like writing, being a dad, and consulting, he studies public policy and community planning, two things that hold the secret to making this world a better place (along with laughter, stories, and swimming).

Special Thanks

The following people were kind enough to read the stories herein while they were still in early stages. They provided me with sound advice in the kindest way possible. I am forever grateful to all of them.

If I left anyone off this list, I beg your forgiveness. It's not that your insight wasn't appreciated. I'm sure it was. But over the many years it's taken to write this book, my mind has deteriorated rapidly. Just know that assuming other people's wonderful ideas are my own helps me maintain the ridiculous delusion that I know what the hell I'm doing.

Michael Adams—read the full manuscript more than once if you can believe it and is one of the kindest men I have ever met (he would have to be). He has given me advice and inspiration to keep writing.

Daniel Conlon—a man who has never been bored a day in his life, Dan provided me with sound and often beautiful medical, theological, and philosophical advice.

Anthony Giardina—read the full manuscript, provided thorough feedback, and gave me one of the nicest compliments about my writing that I have ever received. I just wish I could remember what it was.

Rolando Hinojosa-Smith—hard to believe I got advice on these stories from this amazing man, but it's true, and delivered with his trademark tenderness and profound wisdom.

Jon Hassler—a writer's writer and a great mentor. I miss him dearly, but am grateful his novels and stories will live on forever.

Gretchen Kresl—who not only brought me into this world but taught me to love stories, the importance of character, and the art of a well-placed profanity.

James Magnuson—took time out of his busy schedule counseling writers with much greater talent than me to provide me with constructive advice on my writing.

Cristina Zambrano—had the decency to marry me. Even after reading my writing. She, along with Lemon, are the ultimate inspiration and the reason for everything.

CPSIA information can be obtained
at www.ICGtesting.com
Printed in the USA
LVOW12s0300280416
485680LV00003B/5/P